Blaze™

Dear Reader,

I love geeks. I married a geek. My favorite author is Jim Butcher, and if Joss Whedon or Steven Moffat wanted me to have his baby, I'd be there in a heartbeat. And yes, I've even met the cast and crew of *The Big Bang Theory* and was in heaven.

Where did I meet them? you ask. Why, at the best place in the whole wide world: a convention! San Diego Comicon, to be exact, but I'm a big convention girl. I love the panels, the fans, the corsets and the shows. Which is why I was thrilled to write a story set in the world of geek fandom. And I was really excited to take a normal girl, throw her into a corset and let her strut her stuff, even though she's a little shy and has no idea what she's getting herself into.

Of course, she ends up loving it. After all, who doesn't want to have an hourglass figure and parade around in half boots while guys fall over themselves to talk to you? And if you can find true love along the way, then why not?

I hope you all get the chance to live out your own fantasies someday. My heroine, Ali, and hero, Ken, can attest that it's the ride of a lifetime!

Enjoy!

Kathy Lyons

Kathy Lyons

LIVING THE FANTASY

HARLEQUIN®
entertain, enrich, inspire™

Recycling programs
for this product may
not exist in your area.

ISBN-13: 978-0-373-79719-6

LIVING THE FANTASY

www.Harlequin.com

Printed in U.S.A.

ABOUT THE AUTHOR

A *USA TODAY* bestselling author, Kathy Lyons has made her mark with sizzling romances. She adores unique settings, wild characters and erotic, exotic love. And if she throws in a dragon or a tigress here and there, it's only in the name of fun! An author of more than thirty novels, she adores the fabulousness that is Harlequin Blaze. She calls them her sexy treat and hopes you find them equally delicious. Kathy loves hearing from readers. Visit her at www.kathylyons.com or find her on Facebook and Twitter under her other pen name, Jade Lee.

Books by Kathy Lyons

HARLEQUIN BLAZE

To get the inside scoop on Harlequin Blaze and its talented writers, be sure to check out blazeauthors.com.

Brenda, you made this book awesome.
THANK YOU!

1

OMG I'm going to kill this client!

ALI FLORES LAUGHED as she looked at the text message from her best friend, Elisa. Apparently some guy had hired Elisa's modeling agency to find an actress for him but he couldn't verbalize what he was looking for. Go figure. A guy who didn't know what he wanted in a woman. What were the odds?

Ali was smiling as she texted back.

I'm still coming for lunch. Have to get out of here!

She'd just hit Send when her boss popped his head into her cubicle.

"Hey, Ali, did you proofread that brochure?"

"Right here," she said as she handed over the document. "But I really think the photos could be better—"

"Great. I'm having a terrible time getting those promotional pens out of China. Can you call their customs department for me and get it worked out?"

"Because I speak such good Chinese?" *Not.*

"Because you're the best. Thanks!" And off he went with a wave. She wanted to scream. How the heck was she supposed to navigate Chinese customs? But she didn't say a word. Instead, she grabbed her phone and typed out another quick text to Elisa.

My boss knows exactly what he wants: me, chained to my desk. Until I DIE!

She had to get a new job. Truthfully, she had to get a new life, but what? And how? She dropped her chin on her hand and stared at her computer screen. And as she glared at the blinking cursor, she imagined a knight in shining armor stepping up to her desk to rescue her. He'd take her away to his castle, he'd shower her with jewels, and…and he'd probably ask her to mother his seven screaming brats from a previous marriage.

Not!

Ali groaned and started pulling up all the correspondence with the Chinese factory. But as she worked, her mind kept churning on her own life problems.

Ali believed in happily ever after. Perhaps that was the problem. She didn't just believe in it, she ached for it. She obsessed about it. She wanted it with a hunger that filled her fantasy life to overflowing.

But she needed some way to shape her dreams. It wasn't like knights in shining armor were wandering around Houston looking for her. And she wasn't really a damsel in distress. Truth was, she didn't know who or what she was.

She'd been a quiet child growing up, buried in books because that's what she liked. She and her single mom had been happy up until she was ten. Then suddenly her mom up and married a guy with two sons, both younger than Ali. And if that weren't enough, Mom got pregnant just a few months later.

Ali went from the girl who liked to read to the girl who changed diapers, did laundry and screamed at the boys to stay out of her room. In the end, she escaped to college only to quit when the money ran out.

She'd got this job as a secretary to the head of PR in a hospital. Talk about being unimportant. The hospital saved lives. Her boss kept the hospital looking good so it could save lives. And what did she do? She made sure their booth at a health fair was well stocked with promotional pens. Sure, she wasn't screaming at toddlers anymore, but she was working just as hard screaming at customs or tracking UPS shipments or doing whatever menial task her boss threw at her.

Other people had passions, they had goals and a purpose. She had fantasies about handsome pirates not because she liked pirates but because she didn't know what she did like. And she wasn't going to find out sitting here filling out customs forms.

It was time to make a change. So she whipped out her phone and texted Elisa.

Lunch NOW. We're going to find me a new life.

KEN JOHNSON WAS SEARCHING for a queen. And for some ridiculous reason, he couldn't find one. Maybe because Queen Guinevere didn't exist in Houston. Still, he was determined to try. He was now at his seventeenth modeling agency praying that the woman he sought walked through the door. But so far, he'd been sorely disappointed.

Ken was CEO of Quirky Games, Inc., and he was about to launch a new adventure game that he hoped would take the geek world by storm. But in order to do that, he had to throw a huge publicity campaign that included gaming conventions, comic conventions and even a theme-park opening. And after years of experience in the geek gaming world, he knew that every event hinged on one thing: the actors who played the characters.

Any model could strap on a corset and a sword. Put a babe

in a brass bra and kids would look, but they wouldn't necessarily buy. These days, players needed more than a hot chick before they invested the hours to get fluent in a game. They needed a goal, a challenge and, most of all…a queen.

His queen needed to be divinely beautiful but so approachable that boys would immediately want to talk to her, be with her, play the game for hours just to spend more time around her. She needed to be reserved enough to seem mysterious, and yet so warm that you believed she could strap on an apron and serve chocolate-chip cookies. Sex goddess and Betty Crocker, all rolled into one.

That was the queen he wanted, and damn it, she was nowhere to be found.

"I need a break," he said, shoving up from his chair. He was in the primary conference room of the last modeling agency on his list: OMG Action! But just as all the others, every woman who'd strutted, shimmied or swaggered in front of him had left him cold. Not just cold, but vaguely nauseated. They were certainly beautiful, but the personalities beneath the flawless skin and high cheekbones were arrogant or just plain over-the-top.

The agency owner, Marilyn Madison, pushed out of her chair and teetered on her ultra-high heels. "Mr. Johnson!" she cried, panic in her voice.

Then her assistant—a very sweet young woman named Elisa—offered him yet another folder of pictures. "If you could just tell me what look you're going for, perhaps in this pile—"

"I don't care about a look," he said for what felt like the billionth time. "I need the woman to *feel* right, and these girls just don't." And with that he stomped out the door. He didn't stop until he'd pushed through the doors of the elegant glass foyer, but as the office was on the thirty-seventh floor, he ended up standing in the hallway near the elevator bank.

He toyed with the idea of just leaving the building. He

could be at his favorite comic-book store in twenty minutes. Except, of course, he was an adult today. He had a company and—more important—twenty employees who needed him to make Winning Guinevere into a multimillion-dollar success. Their jobs and his life savings depended on it.

Eight years ago, he'd been fresh out of college with a computer-science degree and a hunger to make it rich. He had a cool game written, and he and his best friend, Paul, had marketed the heck out of it and sold a zillion copies. Quirky Games, Inc. was born. But that was eight years ago. Since then, they'd launched one game after another to only middling success. Winning Guinevere was their last hope, and Ken was pouring everything he had into it. Which meant he had to find the right Guinevere. Without her, he might as well declare bankruptcy now.

He took a deep breath and tried to think. Maybe there was a compromise somewhere. He ran through different scenarios in his mind, but every one just made him sigh. Everything hinged on the woman. He couldn't compromise there. It would compromise everything.

He was on the verge of muttering curse words in Klingon when the elevator doors dinged. He didn't look out of curiosity—his eyes were just focused in that direction. But since his eyes were aimed at the elevator door, he could hardly fail to notice when *she* walked out. Normal height, nice curves and thick dark hair pulled back into a neat ponytail. He caught a flash of flawless skin, high cheekbones and enticing legs that had enough muscle to be strong and enough softness to be sexy. She wore a dress of muted blue and a sweater that covered her curves but didn't hide them.

And none of that made him leap off the wall until he heard her chuckle. Low, throaty and so damn sexy, he felt his jaw drop in shock. It seemed to fill the air and vibrate in his soul. Sexy and *warm*. Chocolate-chip-cookie warm.

Oh my God, had he just found his queen?

He pulled himself together—a lot harder to do than it should have been—and scrambled for a way to introduce himself. Meanwhile, she turned out of the elevator alcove and headed down the hall toward him. Her eyes were trained on her cell phone. That was apparently what had made her laugh because a second later, she did it again.

Wow. He felt this one in his spine, and every part of him leaped to follow her. The words were out of his mouth before he could think twice.

"Excuse me, miss…" he began, but then his voice trailed away. What could he say to this woman?

She looked up, her eyes going wide as she realized she'd been so focused on her phone that she hadn't seen him there. "Oh!" she gasped. "I'm sorry. I should look where I'm going, huh?" She immediately folded up her phone.

"No, no. My fault. I…uh…" He tried his best smile, his mind scrambling. The problem was that as smart as he was—and frankly, he was considered very smart—he'd never been very good at communicating with girls. He wanted to be suave and ended up just looking like a tongue-tied geek. Which was exactly what he was. "I was just admiring your phone."

She blinked and looked down at the cell in her hand. Ken noted with dismay that it wasn't a cool phone. It wasn't even a smartphone, which made it a virtual dinosaur.

"This phone?" she asked.

"Um, no. Actually I was just looking for a way to talk to you."

She smiled. "Bad luck then, choosing to talk about my phone. I'm just grateful it can handle text messages."

He stared at her, lost in her face. Flawless skin was right: like the smoothest latte ever, only with a dusting of gold. She seemed to be of Polynesian descent, which made her look exotic. But what really caught him were her meltingly chocolate-brown eyes. And, best of all, each of her cheeks sported a dimple.

She was perfect. Absolutely perfect.

Meanwhile, she put away her big clunker of a phone while he grabbed for something more to say. "So you must not be one of those ultra-plugged-in people. Internet, social media, a zillion apps just to get coffee?"

She shook her head, but didn't laugh. In truth, she seemed almost shy the way she ducked her head. But her eyes sparkled when she spoke. "Not me. Whenever I check my email, I get junk or more things to do from my boss."

He gave a mock shudder. "Hate that." Even though he was technically the boss, every time he opened his email he ended up with ten more things on his to-do list. Meanwhile, he tried to cover his ultra-slick phone with his elbow. She noticed of course, and gestured to where it was hanging like a lead weight on his belt.

"You seem kinda plugged in, though."

"Um, yeah. You never know when the urge to get a triple mocha latte will hit."

She lifted her chin, her eyes dropping to a sexy half mast as she murmured a long, appreciative, "Yummmm."

His blood went straight south. Not only did she sound sexy, but suddenly her expression sparked all sorts of dark things in his imagination. Meanwhile, she had straightened and was looking down the hall. Hell, he was about to lose her, so he scrambled for another way to keep her with him for just a moment longer.

"Um, really, I was just looking for a way to talk to you." Lord, was there ever a more lame way to approach a girl? Especially since he now realized he'd already said that.

"Talk to me?" she echoed. Then she flushed slightly and smiled back at him. "I mean, hello. Nice to meet you."

He held out his hand, but out of habit, he wiped it first on his pants. He'd spent so much of his adolescence with sweaty, gross hands that it was just an automatic gesture. Then he cursed himself for being an idiot. He was in a suit, for God's sake. And now she was wondering what had been on his hands when it had been nothing!

Mentally he sighed and tried even harder to be charming. He grabbed her hand and shook it too hard. "My name is Ken. Ken Johnson."

"I'm Ali," she said, as she glanced beyond his left shoulder. "And, um, I have a meeting…"

"Oh, right!" He stepped aside, his thoughts whirling. Could she possibly be going into the agency? Was God smiling on him? Could she maybe be a model?

She stepped past him, and he tried not to look like a creepy stalker. But that was harder than it seemed given that he was loitering in the hallway for no reason at all. Then it didn't matter because, *yes,* she pushed through the doorway of the agency.

She was a model and she was *hired!*

He stumbled after her, nearly tripping over himself in his excitement. He made it through the doors right on her heels. She turned at his noisy entrance, her eyes going wide and her lips parting on a sweet gasp of surprise. In the background, Elisa came forward, talking to the newcomer.

"There you are! I'm so sorry—"

"Don't apologize, Miss…" What was her name? All he could remember was Elisa. "Look, Elisa, this girl right here, I want her." Belatedly he realized he couldn't afford to pay exorbitant rates, and he ought to be negotiating. "I mean, assuming she's a reasonable price."

Both women gaped at him. It took him a moment to realize that Elisa had been talking to the newcomer, not him. Meanwhile, Elisa recovered first, her skin flushing a dark red. "Oh, no, Mr. Johnson. I'm sorry. She's not for sale."

He ground his teeth together. Damn it, she was already booked. He turned to the model, trying not to appear desperate. But he was desperate! "How long until you're available? Are there breaks? A weekend or two? I'm sure we could work things out."

He reached out to touch her arm, but Elisa quickly stepped between them. "Mr. Johnson, you don't understand."

He refused to let anyone come between him and his queen. He pushed Elisa aside as gently as he could. Fortunately she wasn't all that stable on her stiletto heels or he might not have managed it. Meanwhile, his eyes were on the woman he wanted.

"What's your normal rate?"

Instead of answering, his queen swallowed, and her eyes darted anxiously between him and Elisa. Uh-oh. Not a good sign.

"Look," he said, "I know this is unusual, but I'm not crazy."

"You just want to buy me," she said, her voice soft. God, she had the most beautiful voice. Just listening to it made everything in him go still.

"Hire you," he scrambled to say. "Hire you. To be my queen."

She blinked at him.

"Mr. Johnson!" snapped Elisa. "She's not our model!"

She wasn't… Oh! "So you're with a different agency?" he asked.

"Um, no," his goddess answered. "St. Catherine's Hospital."

He frowned and looked at her, his body actually lurching as he tried to understand her words. "Hospital? You're a…a…" He looked at her, mentally trying to fit her into the medical profession. Doctor? Nurse? None of that seemed to fit. "Um…"

"I work in the PR department doing events. Health fairs and the like."

"Health fairs?" His queen was…a PR girl? But that was perfect! She was in PR. She knew how to handle—

"Sorry. I'm just here for lunch." She gave him a self-conscious shrug and turned to Elisa. "Are you free yet?"

"Uh…" began Elisa, but then from directly behind them, the head of OMG Action! spoke, her voice cutting through the foyer in strident tones.

"No, she's not!" said Marilyn Madison. "Both of them are coming with me!"

Then the strangest thing happened. All three of them— himself, Elisa and his queen—all groaned at once.

2

ALI FLORES COULDN'T LOOK AT the cute guy who'd tried to flirt with her in the hallway. She'd figured out his problem. He'd assumed she was a model just because she was headed into the agency, and wasn't that just too funny! The idea of her as a model cracked her up. She wasn't tall, blonde or rail-thin. And she certainly didn't have the style sense to do anything like modeling.

Still, she had to admit she was flattered, even if he really needed to get his eyes checked. She had been looking forward to giggling with Elisa about it over lunch when Mad Marilyn saw them. That was their code name for Marilyn Madison, owner of the agency and somewhat of a bitch.

Last week, Elisa had taken Ali out to lunch for her twenty-eighth birthday. It wasn't until they were on their way back to the office that Elisa realized she'd accidentally paid using the corporate credit card. Sure, Elisa had refunded the money into the petty-cash drawer along with the receipt and the explanation, but Ali just knew the madwoman was going to ream them both out at the first opportunity. And now the time had come to pay the piper.

Too bad it had to happen in front of that cute guy she couldn't quite look at.

Ali mouthed the word *busted* to her friend, then turned

around to face Marilyn. Since she wasn't employed here, Ali fully intended to take all the blame. She wasn't exactly sure how she was going to manage that except that she was really good at constructing elaborate cover stories. She'd just have to make sure it was really good.

With that thought in mind, she pasted on an ultra-innocent smile and turned around. First off: start with flattery.

"Why, Miss Madison, look at you! You've lost weight!"

As expected, the woman stopped glaring long enough to shoot Ali an I-know-what-you're-doing smile. "Thank you for noticing," the woman said. "I've always thought you to be unusually perceptive."

Ali blinked. She had? Since when? As far as she was aware, the woman didn't even know her name. Then she had to mentally slap herself. Obviously, the woman was simply shooting back the same insincere flattery that Ali had given her.

"Now come along, you two," the woman said, punctuating her order with a glare at Elisa.

Ali shuddered. This was not good.

Then the woman turned a dazzling smile on the sweet Blind Ken, as Ali had now named him in her mind.

"Mr. Johnson, please, if you would give us just a moment, I'm sure I can work things out just as you'd like."

"But I'd like—"

"Yes," Mad Marilyn interrupted. "I know exactly what you want, and I'm going to make sure you get it. But first, I've ordered some sandwiches and coffee. They'll be up in just a moment. Why don't you wait with your VP in the conference room. I'll be just a moment."

Blind Ken had a VP? Wow, he must be the difficult client Elisa had been texting her about. The guy who wasn't happy with any of their usual models, but couldn't say why.

She looked up at him, and immediately regretted her decision. He was staring intently at her. He obviously wanted to say something but wasn't sure what. She could relate. She spent half her life thinking she ought to say something, but not knowing what would work.

The moment stretched on, and the pressure to say something—anything—built inside her. She took a breath at the very same moment he did, but then Mad Marilyn beat them both to the punch.

"In here please, Miss Flores," she said in a freezing tone.

Nothing to do now but shut her mouth and follow the madwoman into her office. At least Elisa would be in there, too, but one look at her friend's face and she could tell they were both equally clueless about what was going on.

She'd barely stepped into the large room when Marilyn started talking and rooting through files at the same moment.

"Shut the door, Elisa. Have a seat, Miss Flores. We really need to change your name. Never model under your real name. How do you feel about Flowers?"

Ali frowned, replaying the sentences in her mind. Nope. They still didn't make any sense. But Mad Marilyn looked up to pin her with a glare.

"Well? Do you like Flowers?"

"Um, yes?" Who didn't like flowers?

"Excellent." Marilyn pulled out a thick contract, set it down on the desk and started writing. "So your name will be Ali Flowers. You'll have the standard agency agreement, but before I can release you to Mr. Johnson, you'll need some training. Emergency training, if you catch my drift. But lucky for you, I can simply deduct the cost of that from the contract with GQ."

Elisa stepped closer after having closed the door. "I think you mean QG. Quirky Games."

Marilyn looked up and frowned. "What? Oh, right. These games. Ridiculous name. Quirky. Whatever. Now, Ms. Flowers, will you please sign here, here, here, and initial here." She pushed a pen forward into Ali's hand.

Ali barely managed to grab hold of the pen, but beyond that, she didn't move a muscle. She felt like an idiot—and a slow one to boot—but she had no clue what was going on and no interest in signing anything until she did.

So she carefully set the pen down. "I'm afraid I don't understand. Why would I sign an agency agreement with you?"

"So you can be GQ's Guinevere!"

"QG," she corrected. It was the only thing she understood. That they were definitely *not* talking about *Gentlemen's Quarterly.*

Mad Marilyn waved that away with an impatient snort. "Look, I understand you want more money. Don't we all? But I simply can't get you ready in time *and* forgo the usual agency cut. Believe me I'll be earning every cent!"

Ali shook her head. "But I don't want to be a model." The idea was laughable! "And why would you—"

"Marilyn, please," cried Elisa. Apparently, she understood what was going on. "Ali just came here for lunch."

"Well, what has that to do with anything? Look," she said, turning her laser eyes on Ali. "That man out there has a lot of money. He's been looking all over the city for some woman to play his Queen Guinevere in a summer promotional sweep. And now he wants you." She grabbed the pen and pushed it into Ali's hand. "So sign. Then you and I can make a lot of money."

Ali gaped at her. "Guinevere? Me?"

Marilyn rolled her eyes. "Yes, you!"

"But why?"

"Because he's a crazy man! You're not tall enough, you're not trained in any way and you could stand to lose a few pounds."

"Hey!" That was Elisa, not Ali. Sadly, Ali knew everything the woman said was absolutely correct.

"But I don't understand why," said Ali, her gaze going to

Elisa. Sadly, Mad Marilyn wasn't allowing anyone to talk but herself.

"It doesn't matter why, Miss Flowers. It matters that you say yes!" This time she forcibly wrapped Ali's fingers around the pen.

"But I don't know anything about modeling—"

"I'll teach you everything you need to know."

"—and I already have a job!" That last protest was pure reflex. After all, hadn't she just decided she needed to re-make her life? But modeling had never entered her mind as a possibility.

Meanwhile, Marilyn huffed as she sat back in her chair. "Shall I be blunt?" she asked.

As if she was ever anything else! "I'm not a model," Ali said.

"No, my dear, you're a secretary in a hospital PR department."

Ali blinked. How did Marilyn know that? "I manage events, coordinate publicity and logistics. It's an important job!" She said the words, but inside, she knew it really was a lame job. Sure, what she did was valuable, but all it took was an organized mind. She had that in spades. She was valued (at least she hoped she was) but from anyone else's perspective, she was just another cog in a very big machine.

"And now you have a chance to be something better. Something special! A Marilyn Madison Model!"

Ali didn't know how to answer. The idea of her as a model was just too far to go, and yet she was starting to think about it. Could she really be pretty enough to be a model? She wasn't ugly, but she'd never thought of herself as beautiful.

"Think of it!" Mad Marilyn pressed. "Your picture in the paper, screaming fans, cameras, a life under the lights! It's what every girl wants, and it's being handed to you on a silver platter!"

Uh-oh. Wrong thing to say. As Marilyn started speaking,

the reality of what a model had to do started hitting. She'd be put on display. All those cameras! What if she said the wrong thing? What if she did the wrong thing? She would be promoting Blind Ken's product—whatever it was—but if she screwed up then that would reflect badly on him.

"No," she whispered. "No, I can't do that."

Marilyn released her breath on a huff of disgust. Then she shook her head. "Listen to me, Miss Flores. I know this is fast, I know this is a big change. But sometimes opportunity happens like that. It's there and then it's gone like that." She snapped her fingers with a loud crack. "So take it now while it's being offered. Otherwise it's gone." Again, she snapped her fingers and the sound seemed to echo in Ali's head. "Think hard. And think fast."

Then she pushed out of her chair and shot a glare at Elisa. "You're her friend! Explain the situation. Explain how great an *opportunity* this is." She straightened her very tight fitted jacket. "I'll go negotiate your fee." Then she was gone.

Ali waited a long time after Marilyn was gone before looking at Elisa. They were best friends, had been since college when they'd been assigned each other as roommates. They couldn't be more opposite. Where Ali was studious and shy, an introvert with a love of reading, Elisa was vivacious, spontaneous and had a burning desire to be a runway model. After she'd failed a dozen auditions, Elisa decided to use her brain and body a little differently. She interned at Marilyn's agency and was so good at it that Marilyn hired her as soon as the internship was over.

Elisa couldn't be a top model, but she could help other girls attain the dream. And now, apparently, her job was to see that Ali became exactly what Elisa had dreamed of. But Ali just couldn't do it. She couldn't be a model. She didn't know anything about it!

"Don't shake your head, sweetie," Elisa said as she pulled

up a chair. "Let me guess. You're thinking that you can't be a model, not because you aren't pretty enough—"

"I'm *not!*"

"The client says you are."

Ali didn't have an answer to that, so she buttoned her lip.

"You're thinking that you can't stand having people look at you. That you'd be the center of attention and that you'd mess it up somehow."

Ali sighed. "It's not fair of Marilyn to make you talk me into this."

Elisa shrugged. "Don't think about me right now. Let's talk about you."

"I can't be a model!"

"You keep saying that, but what really is stopping you?"

"I have a job."

"And didn't you just text me that you wanted a new one?" Elisa pulled out her phone and paged through to the right text message. "Oh, I'm sorry," she said. "What you actually said was: 'We're going to find me a new life.'"

Ali sighed. Sure she'd said that, and she'd even meant it. "But I can't just change my entire life over lunch."

Elisa shrugged. "Like Marilyn said, sometimes things happen that fast."

"Don't you dare snap your fingers!" Ali groused. Of course Elisa didn't have to. Ali still had the sound of Marilyn's *snap* echoing in her brain. But even as her heart was starting to think of the possibility, her brain was busy coming up with reasons she couldn't possibly do this.

"I'd be a lousy model." She'd spent her life on logistics and organization. It had been a necessary survival skill while managing her three younger siblings. "My skills are great *backstage*."

Again, Elisa just shrugged. "Maybe it's time to learn some new skills."

Sure it was. But modeling? "I haven't a clue what to do."

"Well, that's easy enough. We'll teach you. And besides, you're not going on a runway. You're just dressing up and talking to people. You do that every day."

"I talk to people at health fairs. About finding the right doctor and managing their blood pressure."

"And now you'll talk to kids about a game. Really, Ali, you're incredibly smart. You'll get the hang of it in no time."

Ali tried to picture it. She imagined herself as one of those product girls she saw at health fairs, the ones attached to some drug company. They looked good, but dressed on the edge of too slutty, in her opinion. They were there to draw people to the booth so that they could try a sample of an over-the-counter medication. Or a new arch support. Or something. They were product girls, and…and well, what they did wasn't that hard.

"That can't pay enough compared to what I'm making now."

"Are you sure? That's what Marilyn's out there negotiating right now. And from what I saw, Mr. Johnson wants you bad. That means big-dollar bad."

Ali shook her head, but inside she was thinking. After all, Marilyn was right; every little girl wanted to be thought of as gorgeous, so beautiful people would flock to see her. But as a child she'd been much too shy and awkward to want anyone looking at her. There wasn't any big trauma in her background. She was just more comfortable watching the action than being part of it. She was the girl who made sure things ran smoothly, whether that meant making sure her brothers had their uniforms for the big soccer game or watching the UPS website to be sure the hospital booth arrived at the event stadium. It had taken her a year to be able to function smoothly in a booth, speaking clearly in a crowd without stammering or blushing.

"I can't lose my job," she said. "What happens when the promo sweep is over?"

Elisa leaned back. "What about a leave of absence? I saw the events he has planned. It's three months, tops. Good work for a model."

"I'm not a model." She said the words out of habit, but she was already softening.

"Don't think of it as being a model. Think of it as an acting job."

"Not helping."

"People won't be looking at you, Ali. They'll be looking at Mr. Johnson's queen."

Ali didn't even know how Elisa could say those words with a straight face. "How does a queen act? What if I do it wrong? It'll reflect badly on his game and this agency."

Elisa snorted. "You think too much about other people. Let Marilyn worry about the agency. Let Mr. Johnson worry about his product. You're just being hired to stand around looking pretty. You can do that! Especially if you get paid really well for it."

Ali squirmed. She could tell that Elisa wanted her to say yes. But the idea was so ludicrous. And yet even as she said those words to herself, she wondered if she were lying. Obviously, it wasn't ludicrous. Not if Marilyn could really get her good pay. And yes, Elisa was right. Blind Ken seemed to think she'd be perfect for the job. He was delusional, but that wouldn't stop him from paying her.

"What if I get fired without pay?"

"You won't screw up, and Marilyn's big on up-front pay."

Ali gaped. "Can she do that?"

Elisa shrugged. "Not usually, but like I said: he wants you."

Elisa stopped speaking, waiting while a zillion thoughts spun around in Ali's brain. Elisa knew her well. She knew that she had to think things through. That she hated being bullied. And that...

"One last thing," Elisa said. "Today's text wasn't just out of the blue. You've been ready for a change for a while now.

Just last week you said you were getting frustrated. That you felt you were in a rut. You weren't going to get promoted, you'd topped out your pay at the peon level—" Ali opened her mouth, but Elisa stopped her with a pointed finger. A gesture she'd obviously learned from Marilyn. "Those are *your* words, Ali! 'The peon level.'"

Oh, right. She had said that.

"So maybe this is the shake-up you need, a summer of opportunity. If nothing else, think of it as a paid vacation. You'll only be on a stage a few hours a day. After that, you can sit around in your hotel room and read. Or maybe you'll go to the bar and get a drink. Hang out with your fellow actors. Come on, Ali, are you sure you don't want to try it? Just for a few months?"

Ali shifted uncomfortably in her seat, her mind continuing to race. Everything Elisa said was right. Absolutely everything. But could she do it? There were so many things that would have to work out right. The pay, for one. The leave of absence from her current job, for another.

"Tell you what," Elisa said, proving that she knew Ali was weakening. "Why don't you go out and chat with Mr. Johnson? Find out exactly what he wants. You'll see how easy it will be."

At the mention of Mr. Johnson, Ali felt her face heat. He was cute. She'd enjoyed the short exchange that they'd had in the hallway. He'd seemed real and, well, just her speed. That meant funny and dorky in a nice way. Not the silk-shirt-and-thousand-dollar-suit guys that Elisa usually dated.

She thought about working with him day after day. He wasn't tall, which was great. At five foot six, she hated feeling like a shrimp next to big guys. He had dark curly hair and nice brown eyes, though she'd noticed they were a bit red. As if he was already hours into a too-long day and it was barely one o'clock. But mostly she remembered how he'd made her feel: relaxed. As if he was just as nervous as she was, and so together they'd muddle along fine.

It was an odd thought to have after just a few minutes' conversation, but the feeling persisted. Maybe it was his smile—warm and genuine, but still holding a hint of anxiety. As though he really wanted to make a good impression. Which made her smile because, honestly, what über-rich guy wanted to please her?

In short, the answer was yes. She could imagine working every day with him. In truth, she thought it could be really awesome. She'd just have to stop thinking of him as Blind Ken. He was Mr. Johnson from now on. Her boss…maybe.

"Okay," she finally said.

"Okay, you'll do it?"

"Okay, I'll go talk a little more with Blind Ken."

Elisa snorted. "You cannot call him that. And he's not blind! How many times have I told you that you're way more beautiful than you think?"

Ali shrugged as she straightened up from her chair. Then she rubbed her hands nervously along her skirt and wished she'd refreshed her makeup. "Do I have time—"

The door burst open and Marilyn stomped in looking for all the world as if she was ready to wrestle a bear. "Are you done? Did you sign? Can we go meet the client now?"

Guess there was no time for a makeup refresh. "Yes, I'll meet Mr. Johnson now."

Marilyn froze, her gaze darting to the unsigned contract.

"And then," pressed Ali, "we can decide about an agency agreement."

But first, she had to impress the hell out of Blind—er, Notblind Ken. The CEO of some quirky company. And when exactly had she stepped from normal world into wonderland?

3

Ken didn't know whether to be depressed or dive head-long into a Desperate Act. It was obvious that he had erred badly. Having finally found his queen, he'd assumed she was a model (Mistake number one), stalked her like a psycho creep (Mistake number two), declared he "wanted her" and tried to buy her for a weekend or more (Mistake number three), and then when he'd finally realized his error, he lost the opportunity to explain himself (Mistake number four). Marilyn had whisked the woman away only to return fifteen minutes later to negotiate the woman's fee as if she were bartering the crown jewels.

And in all of that, he got the distinct feeling that his Guinevere—a Ms. Ali Flowers—had no interest in being a model. So now he was faced with two choices. He could either give up entirely—not really an option. Or he could try again with Ali. But how? What to say to explain that he wasn't creepy or insane? And how to convince a hospital PR rep to quit her job to come work for him for a summer? Because he could pay her well, but probably not *that* well.

He was still chewing on that thought when Marilyn finally realized he wasn't going to negotiate any fee until he talked to Ali again. She clicked her teeth shut and pushed up from the table. "I'll be right back," she snapped, then tugged on her short jacket and stomped out.

Which left him sitting in the conference room with Paul, his vice president of marketing, while staring morosely at the table. Fortunately, Paul knew just how to talk to him.

"So, you're sure this is the woman?"

Ken nodded without even taking his chin out of his hand.

"No one else will do?"

Ken shook his head.

"And she's not even a model."

Ken shrugged.

"So basically, we're screwed."

"Unless I can charm her into quitting her job for us."

"Uh-huh. Screwed." Then Paul paused. Ken knew what was coming. Paul was tall, dark and baby-faced cute. Not exactly handsome, but a man who looked and dressed the part of a marketing executive. And if one of them was going to charm Ali, then it would probably be Paul. "Do you want—" Paul began.

"No. Absolutely not. You stay quiet." Both of them were startled by the vehemence in his words.

"Ooo-kay."

"Let me sink or swim on my own here."

Another long pause. "You know you're not being entirely rational, right?"

Ken had no response to that. Of course he wasn't being rational. But apparently, he didn't care. Especially as Marilyn's office opened up and out she came with one sharp-taloned hand gripping his Guinevere's arm.

Ken shot to his feet, yet another mistake (number five) as his chair nearly flopped to the floor behind him. Fortunately, Paul had fast hands and grabbed it. *Get a grip!* Ken ordered himself. But it was hard to hear his own thoughts over the pounding of his heart.

The conference-room door opened and the ladies entered,

Guinevere first. Ken searched her face, hoping for a clue, but he saw nothing that reassured him. Her face was composed, her eyes were alert, but there was a general air of wariness about her. And no wonder. She probably thought he was a total sleaze.

Time to start being charming. He pulled on a smile.

"Hello, Miss Flowers. I'd like to—"

"Flores."

"—apologize. I must have sounded like a… What?"

"Flores. My name is Ali Flores."

"Oh." He could have sworn Marilyn said Flowers. Great, now he was really screwing up. "Um, I apologize. For getting your name wrong and for acting like a lunatic earlier."

She smiled, a soft curving of her lips that did not show teeth. It was a reserved smile, and he found he liked her all the more for it. It softened her face without bowling him over with a polished exterior. It made her feel more real, and he found himself relaxing at the sight of it. She was a normal person. Hopefully, she understood that he was a normal guy—one who made mistakes.

Then Marilyn had to spoil the mood by hauling out a chair and strong-arming Ali into the seat. "Excellent! Now that that's out of the way, let's sit down and talk details."

Ken bristled. He had a Neanderthal reaction to seeing anyone manhandling his queen, even if the man-handler was a woman. But before he could say anything, Paul leaped into the breech. Great, his employee got to be the hero before Ken could do more than glare.

"You know, Marilyn," Paul said, "I believe I need to go over the contract with you in detail. We're not signing anything until I get a few questions answered."

"But what about—"

Paul took Marilyn's arm and physically pulled her off Ali. "I'm in charge of the contract part. My boss is in charge of the campaign and the company as a whole. So you and I are going to talk turkey somewhere else. Now." Then he all but shoved Marilyn out of the room. He was half a step out of the door when he somehow managed to grab hold of Elisa. "You, too," he said. Then he glanced back at Ken and shot him a wink. "Sink or swim, buddy." Then he was gone.

Ken released a slow breath, beyond grateful to finally have Ali in the room alone. But right on the heels of that relief was the knowledge that it was all up to him now.

He tried another smile. "Okay, so now they're gone."

She nodded, but didn't speak.

"So we're clear, I wasn't trying to hire you as a prostitute or anything earlier. I thought you were a model. I was trying to book you—"

"I know," she interrupted. "I figured that out."

"Oh, good. Because I was afraid..." He swallowed. Stay on track. "So I'd like to hire you as a model. But you work at a hospital. Then Marilyn said...well, she said your name was Flowers."

Ali grimaced. "She wants me to change my name."

"Don't you dare!" Then he flushed, belatedly realizing that he had no right to tell her to do anything with her name one way or the other. "I mean, Flores is a great name. And Flowers is a stupid one."

Her lips curved a little more and her eyes seemed to sparkle. "Don't you like flowers?"

Was she teasing him? He didn't know and so he didn't know how to respond. "Um, well, sure, they're pretty and all. And you are, too, so, you know, Flowers would be okay if you really want it. But I don't think you should change who you are. Unless you want to change your name. I mean—"

She laughed, that soft chuckle that pressed every damn happy button he had. Then she pressed her hand to her mouth and her eyes widened. "Oh, sorry," she gasped.

"For what?"

"I, um, I shouldn't have laughed like that."

"No, you should have. I'm falling all over myself today. I'm sorry. I'm trying to impress you and doing such a damn bad job of it."

Again her laughter bubbled up, though he could tell that she was still trying to hold it back. "That's so funny," she murmured.

"Yeah, I get that a lot," he drawled. Usually when he tried to impress a girl. Once again he was choosing *sink* over *swim*.

"No, no!" she exclaimed. "It's funny that you're trying to impress *me*."

He frowned. "Why wouldn't I try to impress you? You're beautiful and charming. And I want to hire you to be my Guinevere."

She sobered and her expression showed true confusion. "But why? Why would you want me?"

And wasn't that just the question of the hour? Paul had asked that, Marilyn, too. He gave the same answer that he'd given them. "Because you fit the part. You're real." He gestured to the stack of model photos on the table. "They're not."

She tilted her head, and he nearly lost himself in the curve of her neck as it met with a nice jaw, swooping up into a perfect shell ear.

"I bet if you'd met them, they'd be real, too."

He snorted. "I have met them. Every single one of them paraded before me all morning. I only have to talk to them for half a minute to realize that they're…well, they're just like Marilyn."

Her eyes widened. "Which part? Mad Marilyn where she decides my name should be Flowers? Or Scary Marilyn where she tells me I've got a dead-end job and that there's nothing special about me unless I take classes from her and lose weight?"

"Don't you dare!" Then again, he remembered that he didn't have the right to tell her what to do and not do. "I mean," he hastily amended, "don't take classes from her.

She'll turn you into one of them." He touched the nearest model photo and pushed it to the opposite side of the table.

"But I should lose weight?"

"What? No! You're fine! And I can't wait to see you in a corset." Oh my God, had he just said that? "I mean…I think you'd look great in a…but not in a skanky way, you know. It's the costume… And you're beautiful in just what you're wearing."

She laughed. "I got it! Guinevere wears a corset."

Thank God. She could understand his babbling. That was a plus as he seemed to be babbling a lot right now. And he really needed to stop. So he took a deep breath and decided to go for broke.

Sink or swim.

"Okay, here's the truth."

She looked up at him, her eyes dark, her skin flawless, and her lips—wow, those lips. He kept getting lost in looking at her mouth. And so, while he was still dazzled, his words began to flow.

"Back in high school there were two girls. Well, there were a lot of girls, but there were these two in particular. Stephanie was flawless. Tall, blonde, volleyball star and a mouth that was always dewy-moist like in those lipstick commercials."

She blinked, and then she absently licked her own lips. His groin tightened at the sight. Her lipstick had mostly worn off, but that just made her more natural in his mind. No cosmetic mask, so to speak. Just her, clean and pure.

"Did you win her?" she asked.

"Geek me? No. But I did hang out around her at a couple parties, listening at the fringe, trying to fit in."

Her lips curved. "I know it well."

"And then one day I went from her crowd to the food table. I was munching on some chips when I started talking to Heidi. She was on the volleyball team, too, but wasn't the star. She had a scar right here." He pointed to a place right above his lip. "We started talking movies, then chemistry class, then philosophy." He snorted. "Well, philosophy the way two sophomores in high school would."

"How long did you two date?"

"That's just the point. We didn't. Not for another year and a half. But suddenly, I realized the difference between beauty and substance. Stephanie's beauty ended up just leaving a bad taste in my mouth because it wasn't real. But Heidi had substance. I could talk with her. We ended up being friends and that was so much better than being attracted by Stephanie's flawless beauty." He gestured to the pile of photos. "These girls are just another pinup, but you're someone I can talk to. I could do it in the hall, and I can do it here. You have no idea how powerful that is. It means the world to me and will to the kids who are going to buy my product."

She stared at him and he just looked back. Did she understand? "But actually, I'm kind of shy."

He smiled. "I know. It's like the difference between a whisper and a shout. I'll tune out a shout. Everyone shouts. But a whisper? Now I'm intrigued. Now I'm leaning in to hear more."

She blinked, and he wondered if he'd caught her. She'd certainly captured him. It wasn't just her unconscious beauty, which certainly grabbed him. It was the way she bit her lip when she was thinking. The way she listened when he spoke. And the way she thought about what he said without just throwing back what she thought he wanted to hear.

"Let me explain what I'm planning." He pulled a series of screen captures out of his folder and pushed them to her. "We're launching this game." He pointed at the cover image of Winning Guinevere.

"Wow. She's gorgeous." She traced the woman's face with a long, tapered finger.

Looking at the design, he made a quick decision. "I'm changing the cover design. Blondes are overdone."

She glanced at him but didn't comment. So he took a deep breath and plunged into his pitch.

"Winning Guinevere is a take on the King Arthur legend turned video game. Players can be anyone in the legend they want—knights, fair maidens, Merlin, King Arthur or Lancelot. They can even be Mordred if they're so inclined."

"The betraying bad guy?"

Ken nodded. "He's there to muck up the works, so to speak. But the core of the story is between Arthur and Lancelot. Who will Guinevere choose?" He lifted the page to show her another picture. "That's you. Guinevere."

She peered down at it. "I don't look anything like her."

"But you *feel* like her. And besides, I'm changing her look to reflect you."

Her eyes widened. "You're not serious."

"I am serious. I can't express how important it is to have the right Guinevere. She will make the campaign that should launch the product that—" He cut off his words. He probably shouldn't tell her that this one product could make or break his whole company.

"And you think I'm Guinevere."

"I know it."

She looked back at the picture in front of her. Then taking a deep breath, she turned the page, looking deeper at the product specifications. "The point of the game is to win…me?"

"You. Your love. Your gifts."

"Seriously?"

"That takes on very specific meanings depending on the player's score. Plus, if they work very hard and do very well, then they get a discount on the purchase of Winning II."

"And kids will do that? Spend hours on the game just to get a game bonus that isn't even real?"

"And a sales pitch for the next game. Yes, they will."

She looked skeptical.

"Trust me. They will because the game is that good. But

I have to get them playing the game in the first place. I have to get them started, and I have to show them you."

"Me."

"Yes, you. Beautiful, sexy as hell, but approachable. Someone who would bestow royal gifts. Someone who understands them and is worth the time and money."

"But I don't understand them. I don't—"

He waved that aside. "You *do* know them, you just don't realize it yet." He huffed out his breath on a sigh. "Look, I know this doesn't make any kind of logical sense, but I know what I'm talking about." At least he prayed he did. "You're Guinevere, and I'd like to hire you to spend the summer with me."

"With you?"

He flushed, his mind going to all the wrong things. "I mean, on tour with the whole crew. It's an entire summer of buses and hotels. You'll get time off, I swear, but it'll be in a different city each week."

He pulled out the schedule to show it to her. Not surprisingly, her eyes widened in surprise. "That's a lot of dates."

"Like I said, at least one every week. We do a different step in the story in every city. We start with Arthur and Guinevere getting married at the first stop, but with Lancelot in the wings. Then the next week there's affection from Lancelot. Next Merlin plays a hand. After that, there's Mordred causing problems. It builds throughout the summer until there's a showdown between Arthur and Lancelot."

"Who wins?"

"You're Guinevere. You get to decide." Then he flashed her a grin. "Well, actually we'll see how the fan choices go. We'll be blogging and getting fan commentary throughout the summer. In the end, the fans choose for you."

She smiled up at him. "That sounds like a lot of fun."

"It is. Exhausting but fun." He pushed another page forward and prayed that she didn't flinch. "This is the pay schedule. We cover all expenses and travel. I'm sorry, but my company is being cut to the bone to do this launch. I'm afraid I can't offer more than this." It was a lie. For her, he'd pay a lot more. He'd find the money somewhere, somehow. For her.

She nodded slowly, chewing on her lower lip as she looked at everything.

"And, um, I'm sorry, but I think the agency will take a cut of that. Marilyn will insist on that. Even if you don't have a contract with her right now, I did meet you here."

"Yeah," she said softly. "I can't see Marilyn giving up her piece of this."

He sighed. After agency fees, the dollars weren't great. Not bad for a summer actor. Good pay, actually. But he had no idea what she made at the hospital. He probably shouldn't have reminded her about the agency fees. Let her think she was getting the whole amount so she had more incentive to say yes. But he didn't want to lie to her, even by omission. Still, he was very aware that he might just have blown it.

"You understand that this is all take-home pay," he said. "We're covering all expenses."

She nodded.

He waited. There was nothing more to say, but God he wanted to. He wanted to beg her to say yes. And as he sat there watching her, seeing the curve of her face, the fullness of her breasts and the feminine arch to her back, he started wanting other things, too.

She flipped through the pages and started reading the contract, her lips pursed as she concentrated. He looked at her lips and starting thinking of other things. What she might also do with those lips. Of what he could do to her to erase the furrows on her forehead. Of what they might do together that had nothing to do with contracts and everything to do with a whole lot of naked wonderfulness in bed.

That's where his mind went and it was wrong, wrong,

wrong! He was her employer—or he wanted to be. So he forced his thoughts down a more professional track.

It took him a while.

"So," he finally asked. "Is this enough to make you quit your job at the hospital?"

She shook her head slowly. "No."

His heart sank.

"But for a summer leave of absence? Yes."

4

THE NEXT FEW WEEKS PASSED in a blur for Ali. The first worry
was that she couldn't get a leave of absence from her job.
That turned out to be the easiest task on her list. Depress-
ingly so. It's not that her boss tossed her out the door. The
man just sighed, asked her if she was sure—she was—and
then approved it. It was a measure of how underappreciated
she was there.

At least her coworkers were sad. Especially as she passed
off one project after another into their hands. Ali consoled
herself with the thought that in her absence, her boss would
realize just how much she did around there. She couldn't bear
thinking about the opposite possibility: that no one would
even notice she was gone. That was just too depressing for
words.

Then there was passing off her plants, getting Elisa to
check in on the apartment, and lastly to convince her family she wasn't insane. She failed in that last task. Her mother
rolled her eyes and asked who could possibly want Ali as a
model. Not the most supportive attitude, but Ali was committed now. And even if she wasn't, there was something that
kept her headed toward her bizarre summer:

She'd started fantasizing. About her multi-cabillionaire
boss. She'd always had a rich fantasy life. After all, she'd

started out as a latchkey kid to a single mom. Plenty of alone time, plenty of time to lose herself in her imagination. That habit had continued well into adulthood where her imagination took on a decidedly mature aspect. And it was no different when she started dreaming about Ken.

It started out simply enough. As long as she was going to be working for the man, she decided to look him up on Google. There weren't a lot of news items on him, but there was a ton about his games. The man apparently was more interested in getting press for his product than for himself. Her kind of guy.

There was nothing in the news stories about him being megarich, but that didn't seem to matter to her libido. In her fantasies, he was über-rich, über-awesome and über into her. It all built off his smile. He smiled just like she did—a little nervous, a little happy, a little puppy dog. It was cute as hell. And the fact that he talked with her—his attention fully focused on her—well, that was an aphrodisiac all by itself.

Most people were kind enough to start by looking at her during the conversation, but all too soon, they were looking away. She didn't know if she was just too boring to hold anyone's attention or if people just didn't have that long of an attention span. She'd learned to keep everything she said to short sound bites. She delivered her information, and then let whoever wander away. But that hadn't happened with Ken. His attention had been like a laser light. At first it had been a little uncomfortable. But now, in retrospect, she really got off on it.

She wondered what it would be like to have him look at her like that during a date. Or better yet in bed. Yeah, her libido didn't work by half measures. She wanted her guy to have that kind of intensity with her as he did *everything* to her.

She'd spent many a happy night picturing his eyes. But then she belatedly realized the man was going to be her *boss*. Oops. But even knowing that, she couldn't stop herself. Didn't matter what she did to distract herself, Johnny Depp morphed into Ken, Orlando Bloom…same thing. Two kisses into her fantasy, and he became Ken. Even Brendan Fraser, who had his own laser gaze, soon became Ken.

She would just have to remember that Ken could be her fantasy man at night, but during the day, he was strictly professional. Which worked great until they had their first face-to-face a couple of weeks prior to the promo tour.

It was a simple evening get-together at the offices of QG. Everyone involved in the tour was there—Ken, looking slightly harassed; his marketing VP, Paul; and five others. Ali arrived late, of course. She was still wrapping things up at work and had been caught in a meeting. So when she walked in the door she was feeling flushed and very *not* together. She *hated* being late.

That was bad enough, but then she got a look at her co-workers. They were all *gorgeous*. Every single one of them. Even Ken who—objectively speaking—was the most average-looking of them all. Even he was oozing sexiness thanks to her nighttime fantasies, especially as his face lit up the moment she walked in the door.

"Ali! Great! I was getting worried something had happened to you."

She swallowed, reminding herself that this was not fantasy playtime. He was her boss, and she should not be wondering what he looked like undressed. "Sorry. Got caught up in a meeting."

"Bad one, huh?" he asked. Lord, there were six other people in the room, but he just talked right to her. Which, naturally, made her libido do a little happy dance, making the rest of her all soft and liquidy.

"N-not bad," she stammered. "Just awkward. I'm unloading all my work off onto other people, and they don't like it."

"I get that," laughed a honey-warm voice behind her.

Ali spun around and came face to chin with a blond god

of a man. Holy moly, she'd known he was gorgeous the moment she walked into the room, but up close he was downright intimidating.

"Hi," the god said in a steadily deepening voice. "I'm Blake, aka Lancelot, on a quest for gold that, thanks to your influence, becomes a noble mission for good." Then he waggled his eyebrows. "I think you get to knight me!"

"Um…hi," she said.

"Yeah," said Ken, tugging her toward a seat. "Everybody, this is Ali Flores, our Guinevere. Blake, you want to grab those folders and pass them out? Thanks. Then we'll go around the table and introduce ourselves. We're going to be living in close quarters this summer, so I hope we can all be friends."

Everyone took a seat. Because Blake was handing out folders, he was the last to find a chair and ended up being the farthest away. That, actually, was a good thing for Ali. He was too beautiful to be real, and she felt a little uncomfortable next to a man who was so much better-looking than she was. Sadly, everyone there was better-looking, or so it felt to her.

Blake was the only male actor. The others were girls of the bouncy, perky type. Blonde, brunette and redhead, they were clearly chosen because they were both beautiful and friendly. Except as the introductions went around, she realized that the blonde was Tina, Paul's assistant and troupe costumer. The brunette was Ashley, aka Morgan le Fey. And the redhead was Samantha, who would be a tavern wench. Ali just nodded, pretending she knew what that meant.

She'd already met Paul, the marketing VP who would double as Mordred, betrayer of King Arthur. And naturally, Ken would play the king.

Obviously, the others were well used to this type of thing. They introduced themselves easily, talked about their acting experiences and the parts they would play, then gushed a little about how excited they were to be here. But when it came time for her to speak, Ali got flustered and tongue-tied. Unlike them, she had absolutely no experience whatsoever.

"Ali?"

"Um, right." She felt her face heat to crimson. "I'm Ali Flores. I'm Guinevere. And…uh…I'm happy to be here." It was a lie. At the moment, she wanted to be *anywhere* but here.

Then there was a long, awkward pause. Rationally, she figured it wasn't really a long or awkward pause, but her imagination expanded it into something hideous. Good God, how was she ever going to learn how to do this in two weeks?

Fear started building inside her, but she kept it locked down tight. She'd already taken a leave of absence from her job, so she was totally committed. She'd just have to learn fast. So she paid extra attention all through the discussion of itinerary, accommodations, the game and costumes. Costumes were the most awkward because, apparently, the models/actors already had a lot of the things they'd need. The girls all had corsets, daggers and leather pants. Ashley had a neck chain that she'd been given as a joke. Blake even had his own sword and fur boots!

What did Ali have? Um…a blouse? Comfortable shoes?

"No problem," Ken said with a warm smile. "That's why Tina's here. She'll get together with you this weekend and get you all fitted."

"Unless we can meet during the week?" asked Tina hopefully.

Ali shook her head. "My last day is next Wednesday."

"That's okay," said Tina in a very perky voice. Was Ali going to have to learn perky? "How about we meet at Spiked Leather on Saturday morning? The owner knows me. He'll give us a good deal."

Ali could only smile and nod. Spiked leather? She didn't remember Guinevere wearing anything that resembled spikes.

"That's settled," said Ken. Then he smiled at her. Lord, if it weren't for that smile, she might have bolted right then.

"We'll need everyone to come next Thursday for the photo shoot. The address is in your folder."

Photo shoot?

"And finally, we're giving each one of you a copy of the game. Read the instructions. Memorize the product specs. And most of all, play it. A lot. Starting Thursday, you're all on my dime. I expect you to spend all that extra time playing the game. When you're not here, you should be trying to win Guinevere. Bring your friends over. Play with them, too. I expect every one of you to have gotten at least to Adept level by the time we leave."

There were laughter and giggles all around. Apparently, for everyone else, finding playtime with the game wasn't a problem. They all had gaming machines and friends who would fall over themselves to play. Samantha even giggled that she was so going to be queen with her brothers this weekend. They were dying to get their hands on this game.

The best Ali could do was paste on a smile. It had been a major accomplishment to hook up her DVR and connect up cable. She didn't know an Xbox from a doorstop. Her brothers would know. They played enough video games, but they were more likely to play the game themselves and keep her out of it. No way did they have the patience to teach her. Besides, they both had jobs now and were busy with their own lives. Hell, what was she going to do? Then Ken touched her arm.

"Ali, do you think you could hang back for a bit? I'd like to talk with you if you've got the time."

"Uh, sure." She might have said more, but at that moment Paul came rushing up, camera in hand.

"I know you haven't had time to have head shots taken, so I figured I'd just get this started here. If you could smile for me?"

Ali tried, but the sick feeling in her gut was getting worse. She obviously wasn't doing it right because Paul dropped the camera and gave her an equally wan smile.

"Hmm, okay. Try this. Just lift your chin. Disdain. That's good. Aloof? Yes." He aimed the camera back to her face, and she belatedly realized it was shooting video, not taking still photos. Over to the side, the others were leaving, but Ali was still able to imagine their disdainful looks as she tried to show one emotion or another as Paul hopped around.

Then Ken stopped the man with a slight touch. "Do we really need to do those now?"

"Well, not normally," Paul said with a slight grumble. "But *somebody* wants game Guinevere to look like Ms. Flores. The sooner we get some digitized images, the better."

Ken shoved his hands in his pockets and looked awkward. "Oh. Right." Then he glanced at Ali. "Sorry. This will only take a moment."

"But—" she began. Too late. Paul had the camera rolling again.

"It's best if I get all sorts of natural poses," Paul said from behind the lens. "Hey, Ali, how do you feel about zombies?"

She blinked. "Um…bad?"

Paul chuckled. "Depends on the zombie, but okay. How about mass genocide? Republicans? Democrats? I'm looking for a strong emotion here."

Ken stepped in. "Let's go with the basics. Chocolate cheesecake."

Ali gave him a grateful smile. *That* she could be passionate about. "I once offered to have sex with the next person who brought me a slice of black silk pie." Then she immediately blushed. Had she said that aloud? "I was…um…I was in my apartment alone with my boyfriend at the time."

Thankfully, Ken clearly thought it was funny. Paul flashed her a grin along with an eyebrow waggle. "And was it everything you hoped for?"

Ali shrugged. Might as well go with honesty. "Cheesecake, yes. Boyfriend, no."

"Okay, last questions," inserted Ken. "Ever seen someone kick a puppy? Trample flowers in the park?"

She frowned. "When I was a kid, we had a pet cat who was a huntress. I did everything I could to stop her, but she still caught things. Mice, bunnies, birds. It was awful the way she'd play with them. It was worse when she ate them."

"Okay, that's gross," Ken agreed. "But it is their natural instinct."

"I know. But it doesn't mean I wanted to watch her do it. Or that I wanted her to gift me with her kills."

Suddenly, Paul dropped the camera. "Perfect! That's enough for the techies to get started with. Thanks, Ali!" Then with a wave, he moved over to the brunette who was just grabbing her coat.

Ali barely had time to remember he'd been filming her when bam, he was gone. It was rather disconcerting.

"He's a high-energy kind of guy," Ken said from where he stood beside her. "Especially right before a launch. He gets really jazzed on all the details and excitement."

She watched as Paul simultaneously helped Ashley with her coat, passed Tina the camera while issuing instructions and still had time to flirt with Samantha.

"How many lattes a day does he drink?"

"Put it this way. I told him to just buy Starbucks. It'd be cheaper."

Ali giggled, pressing her hand to her mouth as she did it.

"Don't cover up," Ken said as he gently pulled her hand down. "I like seeing you smile. Seeing you laugh is even better."

Here it was. She'd been dreading it from the very beginning. It was one of those moments straight out of her fantasies where he had some reason to touch her and then they ended up just staring at each other. In her dreams, it took about two seconds for her to end up in his arms. Another ten before she was in his bed. But in real life, all she could do was look into his eyes and scream at her libido to shut up. No go. She just stood there looking while her nipples tightened and her belly trembled.

Hell.

Meanwhile, Ken seemed equally caught. He just looked at her, his eyes widening. She wondered if it was panic or terror. Part of her labeled it clear lust, but that came from her libido, which made up stuff all the time. She ignored it. And then suddenly, Paul was there, clapping his hands and completely breaking the moment. Ali jerked at the noise. So did Ken.

"Okay, Ken, I've got a zillion details to work out, but I've changed my mind about hanging around here eating dinner with you. I'm doing it at home with brandy and a cigar."

"He doesn't really drink brandy or smoke cigars," Ken said in a low voice.

"I certainly do! But you're right. Tonight is more likely to be hard lemonade. Can't stand being in this building one more second and besides, there's a Bulls game on tonight."

Ali smiled. "That's what my dad's doing tonight. He's a big fan."

"Good man. Anyway, I'm outta here." Tina rushed in with a big food sack and handed it to Paul, who promptly dug inside it. "Which means you get two subs." He tossed the first wrapped foot-long sub at Ken, then the other.

"Hey!" cried Ken as he fumbled to catch the flying food. He got the first, but didn't have a hand for the second. It caromed off his fingers and toward Ali. Thankfully, she had good reflexes. She managed to snatch it out of the air before disaster struck.

Fortunately, Paul had stopped throwing things. He just dropped the rest of the bag on the table. "I won't toss the drinks at you. I know I'd be the one to clean up the mess."

"Damn straight you would," answered Ken, but Paul wasn't listening. He'd already grabbed Tina's arm and was asking her something about latex body paint. Two seconds later,

Ken and Ali were the only people there. Not a problem, according to her libido. But Ali was working hard to be professional, so she firmly squelched the ideas running rampant through her brain.

"Um, you wanted to talk to me?"

"Oh. Um. Yeah. I noticed you got kind of a panicked look when playing the game came up."

She swallowed. "Uh, yeah."

"Not a big gamer?"

She shook her head.

"Ever played WOW? Warcrest? Legend of Zelda?"

She bit her lip and looked down.

"Okay," he said slowly. "You understand, don't you, that I need you to know this game inside and out? How to play, what to do—everything about it that you can learn in the next week."

She nodded, feeling miserable. How the hell was she going to do that? But even as she was about ready to give up the job, her mind started playing out possibilities. Maybe she didn't have a friend who was up on all the major games, but she knew where a game store was. She could talk to the guys there. Maybe they could teach her how to play. And while she was still thinking of ways around her problem, Ken pushed a sub sandwich into her hand. She looked at it then back up at him.

"Eat up," he said. "Because right after this, you and I are going to party in the lounge."

She stared at him, her lust doing a happy dance that was wholly inappropriate. Finally she managed, "Wh-what?"

"Adventure, mayhem, sex!" he quipped as he leaned across the table and snagged the food bag.

She swallowed, not knowing how to answer.

"Don't worry. I'm really not that good at it. Not compared to the other guys. But at least I can make it fun."

"What?"

He turned to her, his eyebrows raised. "We're going to play the game. We've got it all set up in the lounge. I'll walk you through the basics, then we can play it together." He frowned. "What did you think I was talking about?"

"Um...nothing. The game. Of course." Not like her libido was stuck on the word *sex* or anything.

"Trust me. I go easy on virgins."

She had absolutely no response to that.

5

KEN LEANED BACK in the couch, his gaze on Ali. She had her lower lip caught between her teeth as she frowned at the screen. He didn't even consider giving her a hint. First, because he had before and she'd told him quite clearly that she wanted to figure it out on her own. Second, because he had total faith that she could conquer this particular puzzle.

Because he'd learned in about ten minutes that she was smart.

She'd obviously not grown up with video games. Her eye–hand coordination wasn't lightning-quick and she didn't have the fluidity with the game controller that gamers did. So during fight sequences, she was at a severe disadvantage. But this game was as much about smarts as it was about fighting. In fact, he'd made sure the designers put in at least one smart solution to get past every obstacle. Brute force might help, but it wasn't the only way.

"What if I try…this!" She rapidly moved her avatar around and experimented.

He didn't answer. He already knew it wouldn't work, but it was a good thing to try.

"Well, shoot," she said and once again she started biting her lower lip. Even, white teeth. Red wet lip. God, he was hard for her. Hell, he'd been hard for her from the beginning.

Sadly, he was her boss, so he held back. Besides, she was thinking and that was too sexy a sight for him to interrupt.

She grabbed her soda off the table and took another swig as she stared at the scene on the television. Then she thumbed through a few other screens, looking for a clue.

"Wait a minute…" she said.

There! She'd found it.

"Can you—"

"On it," he said, quickly maneuvering his avatar to help hers.

"I'm going to—"

"I'll brace you like this—"

"Now together—"

Bam! The Impenetrable Wall tumbled to the ground.

"Woo hoo!" she crowed, dropping the controller on her lap as she fell backward into the couch. "Damn, this game is hard!"

"You seem to be flying through it."

She looked up at him in surprise. "Really?"

He nodded. "Really."

Then she looked down at the game box. "Well, the game is designed for teens. I suppose I ought to be flying through it, huh?"

He shook his head as he leaned back into the couch right beside her. They were close enough to touch. In fact, he shifted his leg enough that their knees and some of her calf touched.

"That's mostly a violence-and-sex rating. A lot of these puzzles will stump a teenager."

She laughed. "Well, that's reassuring to my ego. I'm smarter than the average sixteen-year-old."

And sexy, too, with her eyes dancing and her lips wet and so close. He wanted to kiss her. She was thinking it, too. Or at least he thought she was. Her gaze had dropped to his mouth and her body had stilled. The air froze in his chest. Could he? Could she?

Guess not because she abruptly looked away. "Gee, um, what time is it?"

Stifling his disappointment, he glanced at the clock on the gaming machine. "One twenty-seven."

"In the morning?" she gasped as she leaped off the couch. "Holy crap! I've got to go to work tomorrow. Er…today!"

He straightened slowly, shoving his hands into his pockets rather than reach for her. "Can you call in sick?"

"On my last few days there? Just because I stayed up too late gaming?" She blinked a moment then released a short laugh. "I never thought I'd hear myself say that."

He smiled. Impossible *not* to smile when she laughed like that. "Well, consider it research for your new job."

"I still gotta say goodbye to the old one first." Then before he could comment, she held up her hand. "And I'm not calling in sick." Then she sighed. "But I may take the afternoon off if I can't keep my eyes open."

He nodded. "Sounds like a fair compromise."

"I'll remember that, boss, if this happens again over the summer."

He was watching her slip on her shoes, noticing the flash of bright red on her toenails, when her words hit him. "Hey, that's not what I meant!"

She laughed. "Too late. You already said it!"

He released a fake grumble then started turning off the electronics. "Wait for me. I'll walk you to your car."

"You don't need to—"

He stopped her with a shake of his head. "It's a safe area, but there's no sense in taking chances. Besides, I need to get home, too."

She stopped arguing, and he quickly closed up the office. A couple of minutes later he had his satchel/briefcase strapped across his chest and together they headed for the elevators.

Fortunately, he'd had enough time to think of another conversation topic. Or perhaps an old one.

"So you don't have a brother or a male cousin or a boyfriend to show you video games?" If he were honest, it was the boyfriend part he was most interested in.

She laughed. "Actually, yes to all of those things."

His heart plummeted. Fortunately, she didn't seem to notice and kept talking.

"Three brothers, all much younger. A ton of male cousins and even a couple of boyfriends along the way. But none of them had the patience to teach me how to play. Not like you just did." Then she flushed. "Was it terribly boring for you? To wait while I figured things out?"

"What? No! I had a great time."

"Liar."

He held up his hand in a three-fingered pledge. "Scouts' honor. I had a great time. I like watching people figure things out." That was a lie. He liked watching *her* figure things out.

The elevator arrived and they stepped in. He let her push the button for the parking garage since he didn't know what level her car was on. Meanwhile, she kept up the flow of their conversation.

"You're a great teacher. And I gotta say that it's a well-designed game."

"Really? What parts did you especially like?"

She paused, eyeing him a little warily. "You really want to know?"

"Of course I want to know! You're a brand-new gamer! If I could figure out how to interest people like you, then my financial woes would be over."

She paused a moment, and her eyes narrowed. "You have financial woes?"

He sighed. "Don't worry. The launch is safe. Let's just say if the game doesn't sell well, then I *will* have financial woes. As in piles and piles of them."

She nodded, and he could tell she was thinking about that. But in the end she shrugged. "Okay, here you go off the top of my head. I really liked the story behind the game…"

She rattled off a couple of the early sequences, surprising him with her answers. At first he thought she was giving him just generic "girl answers" as Paul would say. In general, girls preferred quicker puzzles, less brute force. But then she warmed to her theme, getting more detailed in her comments and critiques of the story structure. By the time they made it to her car, he wanted to pull out a pad of paper for notes.

"Wow," he said, as she finally ended her comments. "That's just off the top of your head?"

She shrugged. "I read a lot. I like fiction."

"I'd like to hear more. Some of your ideas won't work with what we've already got, but a couple of those were brilliant."

She shook her head. "Now you're just stroking me. None of that was brilliant."

"You'd be surprised what a gamer finds brilliant. And believe me, that last idea about the character arc for Guinevere? That was brilliant."

She flashed him a coy smile. "Well, thank you. I'm glad I could help."

They'd made it to her car. It was a little yellow Saturn, and she unlocked it with her fob. The chirp of the car sounded loud in the garage. Exhausted as he was, he still hated to see the evening end. Apparently, she felt something similar because she turned to face him without opening her car door.

"This was a lot of fun. You've got a great game and…well, I just had a ton of fun. Like I haven't had in years."

"Rough couple of years?" he asked.

She shrugged. "No. Not really. Just settled into a rut. I work, I read, I occasionally have lunch with Elisa. I always thought my life would be more exciting. Instead, it's just kinda routine."

"You're shaking things up now. You're going on tour with us."

She smiled. She shouldn't have looked so good under the harsh parking-garage lights, but she did. She looked beautiful. He swallowed, feeling the need to touch her build inside him. "I, um, I really had a great time, too. And I really hope we can play more."

Her eyebrows rose and too late, he realized what he'd said had a double meaning. "More of the game?" she asked.

"Yeah, more of that," he said. And then he just did it. He kissed her. He'd wanted to since he'd met her, and she was right here.

She gasped in surprise, her body stilling in shock. God, this was wrong of him, but he couldn't stop. He stroked his tongue across her lips, tasting the cherry flavor of her lip gloss. Would she open for him? Or was he about to be shoved onto his ass?

She softened. It happened between one heartbeat and another. She was stiff and tight, and then everything in her seemed to give way. He would remember the feel of it until the day he died. The way she just relaxed into his kiss, tilting her head to give him better access and relaxing her body. She might have melted into him, or maybe he just pressed forward, trapping her body against her car. Either way, she opened herself to his kiss and he was quick to take advantage.

He thrust his tongue into her mouth. He stroked her teeth and the roof of her mouth. She teased back, curling her tongue around his and sucking once. That one action sent him around the moon. He framed her face with his hands and kissed her deeper. He ground his pelvis against her and groaned at the way she pressed back. She set him on fire.

Usually, he tried to think about being skillful with a girl. Usually, he tried to figure out what the right move would be. Not with her. He just kissed her. And he wanted to do so much more. So he let his hands move, feeling the silky softness of her cheeks then her neck. She was a wonder of curves, of hard bone in her shoulders and the soft mounds of her breasts.

She broke off the kiss, dropping her head back as they both struggled for breath. But he could not stop touching her. He shaped her breasts, feeling the bumps from the lace of her bra, but finding the tight points of her nipples infinitely more fascinating. Especially when she gasped as he stroked his thumbs back and forth across them.

Her knees softened and her pelvis rocked against his again. He had to touch her skin, so he slid his hands down and quickly pulled up her blouse. Then he slipped his fingers underneath to stroke the quivering silk of her belly. Meanwhile, he was kissing her throat, tasting the curve of her jaw, heating the trembling pulse of her neck with his breath. But he couldn't tell whose heart was beating faster—hers or his own.

He wanted her, so he slid his hands behind her back, fumbling for the catch on her bra. He wasn't skilled with this, and he was rapidly losing his ability to think at all much less perform a feat of manual dexterity. He just wanted to touch her.

"Ken—"

He did it. He popped her bra and quickly slid his hands around for his reward.

"Oh, Ken…" she murmured.

She had great breasts. They filled his hands, her nipples rolled against his palms, and when he held them she began to quiver in his arms. Her eyes were fluttering and her breath came in quick pants. And below she was rolling against him in a way that made him insane with want.

He felt her hands on his pants, but she couldn't find the button. It didn't matter because she hadn't the reach. Not with his hands moving down her skirt. It was perfect for what he wanted. Not too tight. Just loose enough to push up to her hips and let him slide a thumb inside her panties.

She cried out as he touched her and he nearly came. She was hot and wet and so responsive. And as he stroked her, she wrapped one of her legs around him. Just the feel of her surrounding him had him stroking her harder. Faster.

Then she cried out as her body clenched around his hand. It was amazing.

But her movements dislodged his hand. And then he had to hold her up as she continued to climax. He didn't mind. He adored the sight of her flushed skin, the sound of her cry and the feel of her going wild in his arms. No fantasy he'd ever had topped this.

The moment passed. Her tremors eased. The leg she had wrapped around his hips slid slowly to the ground. And she looked up into his eyes. One second she was dazed, her lips curving in wonder. The next second, the joy was replaced by horror. Her gaze darted around, and he suddenly realized he'd just brought her to orgasm in a parking garage.

If he had the strength—and presence of mind—he might have tossed her over his shoulder and carried her to his bedroom. Or the lounge couch. But he wasn't a caveman. He was, in fact, her boss. And what he'd just done went way beyond unethical.

"Oh, no…" she whispered.

"Uh-oh," he said at almost the exact same moment.

Her gaze turned panicked.

"I was out of line," he said, as he took a hasty step back. Oh, hell, he didn't want to do that. His entire lower body screamed a protest at his brain, but he'd already done it.

Meanwhile, she was hastily straightening her skirt, but her bra was undone, which made her breasts jiggle distractingly. He shouldn't look, but damn it, he couldn't stop himself.

"I never…" she began. "I mean, I wouldn't… I don't—"

"I know," he said, forcing his gaze up to her face. "I've never either. Not…" He gestured weakly to the empty parking garage. Geez, he hadn't even had the decency to hit on her in the lounge. He'd pressed her up against her car. What the hell was wrong with him? He rubbed a hand over his face and tried to find something to say—something to do—to salvage the situation. Sadly, all he could think of was ways to press her back up against her car while she wrapped both legs around him and he—

Stop it! he ordered himself.

She was reaching behind her back. Obviously more dexterous than he was, she got her bra fastened in record time. And then she was just looking at him, mortification coloring her skin a dark red. Damn it, he still found that stunningly gorgeous.

"I'm so sorry," she whispered.

He wasn't exactly sure why, but those three words crushed him. He understood what she was saying. She hadn't meant for that to happen. She knew he was her boss and that what they'd just done was wrong on so many levels. But some part of him thought it had been right. Really right and really good. That same part was hoping she'd want to do it again soon. Maybe even in a bed or at least inside a building. In fact, he wanted it with a passion bordering on insanity.

But she'd said she was sorry. And from the look on her face, this was never, ever going to happen again. Which really hurt part of him even while his rational mind told him she was right. This couldn't happen again.

"Look," he said, as he took another step backward. "It's no big deal," he lied. "We're two consenting adults. Your employment contract doesn't begin until next week anyway, so I'm not exactly your boss yet."

"Right. Right," she answered, though he had no idea if either of them knew what they were saying.

"So," he continued despite his brain's warning to shut up. "So we'll both just pretend this never happened. It doesn't have to affect anything else, right? It was fun. It…um…it happened. No big deal."

She swallowed. "No big deal," she echoed.

"So, um, you're at your car," he said, gesturing to the obvious. He was still backing away, but this time he was trying to distance himself from his own stupid words. "Mine is up a level, so I'm…uh…" He pointed at the elevator.

"Right," she said, flashing him a weak smile. "Good idea. I need to get home anyway." She fumbled at the car door but managed to wrench it open.

"Home. Good idea," he said as he accidentally backed into a concrete post. "Ow."

"Watch yourself," she said with a too-high laugh. Then she practically jumped into her car and slammed the door. By the time he'd straightened off the post, she'd started her engine and was shifting into Reverse.

But she didn't move her car. Instead, she paused and looked at him. It was as if her whole soul was in that look. He could see everything there—the panic, the embarrassment, but there was a flash of joy, too. At least he prayed there was. He really, really hoped that she'd enjoyed what they'd done. Because he certainly had.

Then the moment was over. She ducked her head and nearly squealed her tires in her haste to back out of her space. Three seconds later, she was gone.

6

"HE KISSED YOU? Oh my God!"

Ali flushed. She was talking to Elisa, unable to keep from confessing what she'd done. "Um," Ali hedged. "He did a lot more than kiss me."

Elisa's eyes went round. "All the way?" she gasped.

Ali shrugged. "For me. Not for him."

"He didn't…?" She paused and then her mouth gaped open. But all too soon, her eyes started sparkling with laughter. "Um, really? How very… um…self-sacrificing of him."

"Elisa! This isn't funny!"

"I'm not laughing," she said, even though she was giggling between every word. "Well, not much. Actually," she said as she shifted to prim, "I think it's noble of him. Making sure you had a good time and all. You did have a good time, didn't you?"

"Well, yeah! A really, really good time."

Her friend squealed. "Or should I cry, 'Score!'"

Ali threw a nacho chip at Elisa then dropped her chin into her palm. They were in her kitchen trying to eat the food still in her apartment. That meant stale nachos with questionable bean dip. Frozen veggie burgers that were equally inedible when microwaved. Steamed vegetables that they'd already eaten because they'd wanted to begin with something healthy.

And now it was time for the final serving: chocolate-fudge ice cream.

"Stop laughing and tell me what to do!" Ali ordered as she went for the ice cream and two spoons. Forget bowls, they were going to dig straight into the carton.

"Do?" Elisa shot back. "Do it again if you can! And maybe let him enjoy himself, too!"

"He's my boss! He's your client!"

Elisa sobered. "Well, okay, so that is a hitch. But actors often bunny-rabbit around."

Ali handed her a spoon and popped the top off the carton. "Bunny-rabbit?"

"Yeah, sleeping—"

"I know what you meant. And besides he's not an actor. *I'm* not an actor."

"You are for the summer."

Ali sobered, recognizing her *real* problem when it was spoken aloud. The truth was that sure, it was unethical to sleep with one's boss. But people did it. And, as he'd said, they were both consenting adults. The real problem was that this was just for the summer. "So let's say we, that he and I—"

"Mambo the night away?"

Ali groaned. "Yeah, let's say we do that. What happens when it ends? What if we're still on tour? What if it ends when summer is over?"

Elisa gaped at her. "You've only had one spectacular moment in a parking garage. And now you're already on relationship-ending disasters?"

Ali sighed. She couldn't help it. She thought about things like that. It was the bad side of having a rich imagination. If she and Ken pursued a relationship, then what happened next? Her imagination took the what-if from hot sex to relationship to disaster. Three easy steps in a variety of different ways. "Any way I look at it, it's a bad idea. Besides," she said as she stabbed her spoon into the ice cream, "I don't bunny-rabbit."

Elisa sat back in her chair and looked at her with a suddenly serious expression. "No, you don't. So why did you?"

Ali stared at the scoop of ice cream and wondered if she should confess everything. She was still thinking when Elisa decided to start asking questions.

"Let's start with the basics. What's he like?"

Ali smiled. "He's cute. I think he could be hot with the right clothes and stuff, but mostly he's funny and comfortable. You know, the kind who wears a suit because he has to, but it doesn't quite fit perfectly. The first thing he does is strip out of his jacket and tug at his tie. And he's always running his hand through his hair so it's constantly messy in an adorable kind of way."

"We'll put that down as cute. Geek cute, but cute nonetheless. He runs a company, right? So he's rich."

Ali shook her head, remembering his comment about financial woes. "It's a small business, which means he's got the potential to be really rich. Or really broke."

"Hmmm." Elisa grabbed a pen and notepaper from the counter. "We'll put that as neutral."

"We're not doing a pro/con list about sleeping with my boss."

Elisa looked up with a grin. "Of course not. That would be tacky. We're doing a pro/con list about your boss, period. Whether you sleep with him or not is your choice."

Ali groaned, but Elisa was undeterred.

"Next question, is it about the sex or do you just like hanging out with him?"

"It is not about the sex!" Ali cried. But inside, she wondered. Because, of course, she had been fantasizing about him from the day she'd met him. She'd gone into that meeting strong in her determination to act professionally. But then they'd started playing the game, and she had such a great time. Plus it had been really late, so her defenses were down. And

then he'd looked at her, all intense and hungry, and…and…
"And he's a great kisser."

"Ah-ha!"

Ali started. Oh, hell, had she said that out loud? Apparently so because Elisa was busy writing that down in the pro column.

"Let's get a little more specific," Elisa said.

"You just want gory details."

"Damn straight. So give. If it's not about the sex—great kisses and all—then why do you like hanging out with him?"

Ali chewed on her lower lip as she thought. "He's smart, but he doesn't talk down to me like my brothers do."

"Your brothers are teenage dorks. Leave them out of this."

Ali nodded. "Okay, Ken listens to what I say and he knows just what I'm thinking. Or at least it seems like he does."

"So were you thinking about kissing him? Were you thinking about doing *more* with him?"

Ali didn't answer, but her flaming cheeks were more than enough to set her friend off into another squeal of delight. To which Ali responded by grabbing the ice-cream carton and putting it away.

"Hey! I wasn't done!"

"Yes, you are. Especially if you can't do anything but squeal. This is a real problem. He's my *boss!* There's no way a summer fling can turn out well."

Elisa lifted up the pro/con list and waved it in the air. "But you like him. As in really, really like him." She pushed up from her seat and went to give Ali a hug. "Look, I know you're Miss Ethical and all, but you're about to get paid to dress up in a costume and smile pretty. It's a summer funfest. Enjoy it."

Ali shook her head. "We're going to be living in really close quarters for the next three months. I can't even read his emails right now because I'm so embarrassed. How am I going to spend the next three months with him?"

Elisa sighed. "What did he say? After the…um…"

"Fireworks stopped?"

Elisa giggled, then promptly covered her mouth. "Uh, yeah. What did he say?"

"That we were consenting adults and that we should just pretend it never happened."

"Ouch." She wrinkled her nose. "Do you think it was bad for him? As in he didn't like it?"

Ali shrugged. "I don't know. I mean, he seemed to be enjoying it. Not as much as I was, but…" She groaned and dropped her head into her hands. "I can't believe we did that in a parking garage!"

"Oh, give it up. It's not such a big deal. He's not forcing you, is he?"

Ali's head shot up. "God, no!"

"And you're not going to sue him or anything."

"I loved what he did with me." Again her cheeks heated to crimson. "Why would I sue?"

"Then if it happens again, enjoy it. Don't look for problems where there aren't any."

Ali shook her head. "It's too much. It's too awkward. I'm going to be with him for three months. What if he hates me after one?"

Elisa shrugged. "Then you'll know that there are a lot more cons than pros on this list. You'll come home, see if you can pick up your old job earlier than expected and go on knowing that you tried something different."

"I can't."

"Ali! Weren't you the one complaining that you were in a rut? You're going to be a queen all summer, and being paid to do it! Kick loose and enjoy the ride!"

"But—"

"No buts! You want my advice? Here it is—act professionally around him. Just like he said, pretend nothing happened. But if he goes for more again—and you want more—then let it happen. See if the pros keep piling up. Who knows, this could be the best summer of your life!"

Ali bit her lip, knowing that Elisa was right. But she also worried about…well, about so many things. "It could all go horribly wrong, you know."

"Or wonderfully right. Ali, take a risk," she added as she grabbed the dishes and headed to the sink.

"Okay," she finally said, not sure whether she was agreeing to act professionally or to let something else happen next time she and Ken were alone together. Lord, how was she going to spend a summer acting professionally around Ken? It was hard enough when she'd only been fantasizing about him. Now she knew from experience just how awesome he was.

As she mulled over her dilemma, the phone rang. It was a number she didn't recognize, and her heart sped up to triple time in the hope/fear that it was Ken. But she couldn't keep hiding—not from his emails or his phone calls. So, taking a deep breath, she pressed the button to answer.

"H-hello?"

"Hi, Ali! Glad I caught you!" It was Tina, and Ali released her breath on a whoosh while she tried to calm her heart.

"Hey, Tina. What can I do for you?"

"Well, I managed to get you an appointment at my friend's salon. We've got some great ideas about your hair and I wondered if you could come now?"

"Now?" she gasped. "As in right now?"

"I know it's last-minute, but Marissa knows just what we want."

Ali shrugged. She'd signed a contract, after all. "Um, sure. You're not going to shave me bald, are you?"

Tina released a trill of laughter. "Of course not! You'll like it, I swear. And if you want, she'll give you a good deal on a facial, too. You know, to spruce up the pores before we start burying them under all that stage makeup."

"A facial?"

"I do one before every launch," she said. "It's my make-me-beautiful ritual."

"I've never had a facial before."

"Well, then this will be a special treat. I'll go ahead and schedule it for right after the dye job."

Dye job?

"See you soon! 'Bye!"

ALI GOT HER HAIR DYED. Not all of it. Just a shock of red down beneath her right ear. It took her about eighteen hours to adjust to it, but by the end of the next day, she loved it. Her mother, of course, thought it was appalling and cheap, but she did say that Ali's face glowed. She had to admit that the facial had been well worth the cost. Her skin felt cleansed and polished. And if it didn't, she had nearly two hundred dollars' worth of new face products to make sure that her skin felt especially pampered throughout the summer. Fortunately, QG paid for most of that.

Tina, of course, thought it had been an excellent purchase and wasted no time in discussing the makeup products that Ali also used. Fortunately for her pocketbook, Tina had all the stage makeup Ali would need. Not so fortunate, her date at Spiked Leather came up way too fast for Ali. She'd barely gotten used to her new hair when she walked into the leather shop.

Spiked black leather wasn't even the half of it. She also saw whips, chains and studs, all tooled into leather attire. She walked slowly into the shop, feeling as though her eyes were triple-wide and trying to envision herself in any of these things. Utility belt—she could do that. Leather pants, probably, assuming she didn't look like a cow in them. Cuffs and dog collars? Only if she had to. Leather pasties and all other variety of nipple or breast attachments—no. Same went for the female version of the codpiece. No way was she wearing a leather bikini or…well, she didn't even know what some of those things were.

"There you are!" Tina cried from the very back of the store as she waved Ali deeper in. "I've already gathered what I'd like you to try on. Don't panic. We're not doing any S&M stuff. Just corsets and the like. Fortunately, you're a real-world size. That makes buying off the rack so much easier."

"Real-world size?"

"Yeah. Sometimes trying to find stuff for models is like trying to make a toothpick look sexy. It looks really hot on camera, but it's all specially designed. And since we're not going to spend much time on camera, it's more about personality anyway."

Was she trying to say Ali was fat? No, no, of course she wasn't. But Ali couldn't help but be self-conscious about those extra pounds around her belly and creeping onto her thighs.

"Okay, I guess," she said. "What do you want me to do?"

"We'll start with the basics," she said as she led Ali into a dressing room. "Put on the white shift—that's the silk dress there—and we'll put the corset on top."

Ali held up the simple white gown. "Silk?" she asked.

"Last launch we did, I put the girls in polyester outfits that looked really pretty." Tina shook her head.

"Bad idea?"

"About a third of our events are outside. In the middle of summer. Trust me when I say, you want only natural fibers next to your skin. Unless you enjoy heat rash."

"Silk it is," she said as she ducked into the dressing room. Tina was right. The silk felt heavenly against her skin, but the dress just seemed to hang there. There was very little shape to it. And as much as she enjoyed the basic sheath dress, she'd always thought she was too curvy to wear it.

"Um…" she began.

"Come on out, and we'll start trying on the corsets."

Ali stepped out, but was immediately stopped by Tina.

"No, no. You can't wear a bra with a corset. That would just be silly!"

Of course it would, Ali thought as she rushed to pull off her bra. But then she was swinging free, so to speak, which in her mind meant swinging low beneath the sack dress.

"Um…"

"Trust me, Ali. Come on out."

Okay. She could do this. After all, it was just Tina out there. She hadn't seen any of the store staff when she'd walked in. Or at least none at the back.

Sadly, the moment she stepped out of the dressing room, she realized her mistake. There were other staff here. Two, to be exact. Two tattooed, pierced and Gothed-out guys in black. One was lanky, the other huge. As in motorcycle-gang huge.

Ali paled, but there was no time to run. Tina grabbed her and said, "That's perfect with your skin."

Ali looked down. The pale white did indeed look pretty right now in the middle of spring. "But I tan really, really easily. A month from now, every exposed skin cell is going to be brown."

"How brown?"

"My last name is Flores. You tell me how brown is too much and when I hit it, I'll start putting on sunscreen."

Tina pursed her lips. "Good to know, but you know what? I like a little ethnicity in my queens. The gaming world has way too many golden-haired Galadriels."

"The elf princess from *Lord of the Rings?*"

Tina nodded and flashed a smile. *Oh good,* thought Ali. *I got one right.* But that was the last moment of feel-good she had in a while. Especially as the guys came forward, each with a leather corset in his hands.

Tina grinned. "Aren't they pretty?"

The corsets or the guys? It was hard to tell because though Ali didn't personally go in for tattoos, Tina might be all over that kind of kink. Especially since the big guy was all muscles and ink.

"Ever put on a corset before?" Tina asked.

Ali shook her head.

"Well, welcome to your crash course. Actually, it's pretty easy. You just raise your arms." Ali did. "And then we tie you in."

Turns out Tina wasn't lying. It was really easy to wear a corset, assuming she didn't need to breathe. Because not only were the tattooed guys kinda hunky, but they were also pretty damn strong. Even the lanky one had the pull strength to completely defeat her ribs. Ali was strapped in, her ribs compressed and her breasts lifted from below. Then Tina had her turn this way and that as she snapped some photos. Two minutes later, the laces were untied and Ali could breathe. But then another leather contraption appeared.

Who knew there was such variety in corsets? Forget decorations, of which there were a zillion. Under the breast, over the breast, long line, short line. Then there was her personal nightmare: the W lift where the boning went under her breasts was like the hardest underwire ever. But that felt better than the big U that smooched her together so that her breasts seemed to meet right under her chin.

But on the upside, she did have quite a pretty waist when she was in one of those things. On the downside, someone else would have to put on her shoes because she couldn't bend over to do it. And then, suddenly, it was over. Or at least that part was.

"That's the last of the corsets. Let's look at the boots."

Finally, Ali let herself smile. Boots were something she liked.

Except, of course, she hadn't thought about *queen* boots. Apparently, Guinevere wore spike heels sharp enough to kill someone and high enough for her to kick an elephant.

Ali had never thought of herself as particularly clumsy.

She wasn't an athlete, but she could shoot a basketball and hold her own against her much younger brothers. She'd run a marathon, too. But apparently, that was nothing compared to walking around in five-inch spikes.

"Um, didn't Guinevere wear short gold sandals or something? I feel like I'm on my tiptoes on stilts."

Tina grimaced. "Yeah, those aren't going to work for you. Not with the platforms. How about—"

"Holy cow. My queen, you've ascended to the heights!" said a deep voice from behind her.

Ali spun around. Too late she realized she was spinning in shoes that turned her into the Empire State Building. "Oh shit."

Ken dashed across the small shoe space, half catching her, half overshooting and barreling into her.

"Oh crap!" Ken said as they teetered together.

Thank goodness for big tattoo guy. All he had to do was hold out his arms as the two of them fell against him. Sadly, Ali had landed on top-ish. Ken was squashed between her and the big guy. She scrambled to get off of him, but it wasn't easy in those boots. In the end, Tina had to give her a hand, laughing the whole time.

"Definitely not these boots," she said. Then she turned to Ken. "And now that you're here, we can get down to the real decisions. Meanwhile, Ali, why don't you get out of those boots and into those pants?"

Ali bit her lip, doing her best not to speak. But the words came out anyway. "Uh, hi, Ken," she began. "I didn't realize you were coming."

Ken flashed her a quick smile that looked a little awkward. Good, because Ali was feeling *really awkward.*

"Uh, hi. Yeah. I've got final say on the costuming."

Meanwhile Tina was booting up her iPad. Apparently, all those photos that she'd been snapping had already been loaded onto her pad. Ali peeked over the woman's shoulder to see a spread of herself in all those corsets and boots. And now…pants?

"Uh—"

"Just put on the pants," said Tina. "And don't bother with your bra. The corsets will come next."

Great. She was going to be swinging free right in front of Ken. And even worse, given how tight these leather pants were, he'd have a really good idea of exactly where every piece of candy she'd ever eaten was stored on her thighs and rear.

7

KEN LOST HIS ABILITY to speak. He'd known today's costuming meeting was going to be difficult. Usually he enjoyed picking out outfits with his female models. They loved the shopping, and he was able to direct them to the subtleties of what he wanted them to project. And it was a great way for him to get to know his models. If they gravitated toward the spikes and oohed over the sales guys' tattoos, then he knew that they would work best as steampunk models. If they fidgeted in black leather pants and tugged the corsets higher, then tavern wench was more their speed. Those costumes were equally fun, but the fabric tended to cover things more securely.

But what did he say to Ali? How did he even *look* at the woman without thinking how amazing she had been during her climax? He knew her taste and her scent. And he'd spent the past three days alternately planning ways to get her naked or creating elaborate schemes to keep them apart. He was her boss and he had a strict hands-off policy with all his actors. It just complicated things too damn much. Plus, his entire company was riding on the successful launch of this game. Why would he jeopardize that by having a relationship with one of his employees? Forget the problems it could cause to the launch, it was just too distracting for him right now. His company was at stake!

And yet, the night they'd spent playing Winning Guinevere together was the best night he'd had in years. Years. He didn't want to give that up—to give her up—just because his company was at a very crucial point.

It was maddening, and now he was looking at her in black leather pants that hugged every inch of her curvaceous body. And all he could think—beyond the obvious *I have to bed her now*—was how was he going to hide his total infatuation with this woman?

"Well," said Tina as she tapped the pen against her lips. "Those pants rock, but I'm not sure they're quite what we're looking for in Guinevere."

Ali swallowed nervously, her gaze hopping between the mirror and everyone else's faces. She couldn't quite meet his eyes, which was fine since he was having trouble looking up from the sweet line of her bottom and her muscular legs. And if he dragged his gaze upward, it was to see her breasts as they moved so distractingly. His thoughts—what there were of them—were distinctly X-rated.

Beside him, one of the sales guys laughed in appreciation. "Depends on what kind of Gwen you're going for. Lady of Pain, Queen of Spank Me. Or how about—"

"Not doing S&M," interrupted Ken before he got even *more* images in his head. "Let's go back to the shift and corset look. Show me those pictures again."

Tina nodded, but Ken couldn't stop himself from watching Ali as long as possible in those pants. He saw her nod and head for the dressing room, but not before she stroked her hand along her thigh. She liked those pants, he realized, but she was too professional to say so.

Normally he had trouble stopping the models from expressing their opinions. But that was one of the reasons he'd chosen Ali for this role. She was so reserved. Which told him he'd have to ask her for her thoughts.

"Ali," he said, freezing her in her tracks. *Don't look at her breasts. And not at her ass either!*

"Yes?"

"I'd like your opinion. You've played the game." Oops, shouldn't have brought that up. Her skin immediately flushed red. His probably did, too. "What do you think would be best? Keep in mind that we're appealing to teens, primarily."

She bit her lip, obviously thinking. Her gaze scanned the rack of clothing she'd already worn, then she finally answered. "You want classy sexy."

"But warm. Approachable."

"A hot older sister who is bringing you cookies and asking you very nicely, very sweetly, if you might please go on a quest for her."

He nodded. She understood things perfectly.

"Then give me a long shift—"

"We need to see your legs." Oops. Had he said that out loud? The truth was *he* wanted to see her legs.

"Right. Draping in back, short in front."

Tina started typing. "I can do that."

"Then a corset to give me a waist."

One of the sales guys perked up. "Red leather to match the shock in your hair."

She blinked, but nodded. Apparently she'd forgotten the totally hot change to her hair. "Perfect touch," he inserted as he glanced at Tina. "Great idea."

Tina flashed him a grin.

"So we've got the sexy," he said. "What about queen?"

Ali shook her head. "That comes with jewelry or trim."

Tina frowned. "I can get you a crown that drops across your forehead."

Ken started thinking. "King Arthur gives her the crown at the first publicity stop. Next stop has Lancelot giving you…"

"A necklace," inserted Tina.

"Right. Small fight between Lancelot and Arthur at stop

three, Merlin stuff stop four." He shook his head. "She's going to be buried in jewelry if we're not careful." Ali was too sweet to be covered up in all that stuff.

Tina frowned and looked up. "What about a weapon? A dagger or something. I mean, she's a warrior queen, too. Especially as the tension heats up between Arthur and Lancelot."

Ken smiled. "I like that." He looked over at Ali and knew she could be fierce. Someone just had to bring it out in her.

Meanwhile, Ali wasn't so sure. "But you want warm, too. Chocolate-chip-cookie warm."

"That's you," Ken said. "That's totally you."

She shook her head, obviously doubting him. "That's in the footwear. Fun, flirty…" She sighed as she looked at a pair of thigh-highs. "It's stuff I already have."

God, what he wouldn't give to see her in those boots. "Well, we do have those three steampunk days. That's the week when Lancelot and Arthur go to war. Guinevere needs to be a lot more kick-ass then. Plus, it'll be an adult crowd."

Tina looked up, her eyes narrowing. "You're thinking about those boots over there, aren't you?"

Ken tried to put on a neutral expression while, over to the side, Ali flushed an adorable pink. No way could he resist seeing her in them now.

Fortunately, the sales guy knew his job. He'd already disappeared to get a pair from the back. Five minutes later, they had the look. An over-the-breasts corset, shift and those beautiful thigh-highs.

"Wait!" said Tina. "Ali, take off the shift."

Ali blinked. "But—"

"Just corset and boots. Here, put on these." She tossed her a pair of black tights that were designed for just this purpose.

"Uh—"

"Trust her. Do it." That came from the sales guy and Ken flashed him a look of sheer annoyance. It came from pure jealousy. He didn't want any other man giving Ali suggestions like that. Or seeing her in an outfit like that. But he didn't disagree. He was rock-hard wanting to see it himself.

Ali nodded slowly, then disappeared back into the dressing room. It didn't take her long.

"I need someone to tie this tighter," she called from the dressing room.

"I got it!" Both sales guys were on their feet, but thankfully Tina got there first.

"*I've* got it, boys." Then she ducked into the dressing room. Two aeons later, Ken heard her satisfied grunt. "Yeah, this will definitely work for the evening ComiCon events."

Ken's mouth went dry. Fortunately he didn't need to speak. Tina would bring her out in a sec—

Holy moly. That definitely took Ali from PG to R. And in his brain, they'd gone straight to XXX.

Beside him, one of the sales guys whistled.

"What do you think?" asked Tina.

Ken had to swallow twice before he could speak. In the end, he could only manage two words: "Buy it."

ALI HAD A FEW DAYS to get used to the idea that she would be walking around in a leather corset for part of the summer. It almost kept her from obsessing about the way Ken had looked at her when she was wearing that outfit. The sales guys had been horny. That much she could tell. They'd looked at her with a slick kind of smile and she had immediately looked away. That kind of attention she did *not* like.

But she hadn't been able to resist peeking at Ken. He seemed like he wanted to jump her right then and there. That was frightening enough for her, but he seemed equally freaked out by the thought. His gaze had dropped to the floor, but then a second later, he was looking back at her. She saw him swallow—twice—and didn't that just do wonders for her self-esteem?

That costume—and the way Ken had looked at her—made

her feel sexy. Like a woman who was proud of her body and wasn't afraid to own herself and her clothes. She'd never felt that way before, and she relished the idea of it. Suddenly she was Sexy Ali. And whenever the joy of that started to fade, all she had to do was bring up the memory of Ken staring at her with hunger in his eyes and she was right back to feeling amazing.

That gave her the confidence to sail through the photo shoot where she did *not* wear the catsuit. Phew! It kept her excitement alive as she closed up her apartment and loaded her bags on the bus. It even had her smiling all the way up until she checked into her hotel room the night before their first event.

They were doing a small event. Just a gamer group in Dallas. There was going to be a party at a comic-book shop, and not even a big one, according to Tina. Samantha as a tavern wench would begin working up the crowd, playing off Paul, who would be snide and cynical as Mordred. Lancelot would wander through, but he was just there to help build anticipation for Guinevere and Arthur's wedding. Beyond the obvious "I wed thee, King Arthur," Ali's only job was to notice Lancelot. As she wandered through the crowd, she was supposed to be obviously interested in the handsome knight.

Ali had memorized her lines on the bus, so that was pretty easy, assuming she didn't stutter her way through her part. After that, she was supposed to mingle, talking up the game or just plain talking. That was it. Basic booth work with the occasional look at Lancelot. And so she kept reminding herself as she paced her hotel room. Booth work. She'd done it dozens of times. Of course, this time she'd be in a corset and half boots, but still. Easy peasy.

She was halfway to a panic attack when a soft knock sounded on her door. She nearly wiped out tripping over her own shoes in her haste to get to the door. Anything for a distraction.

And what a distraction! Ken was there, his hair looking even more rumpled than usual. His jeans and faded T-shirt looked comfortable on him. And for the first time she noticed that there was some muscle definition on his arms. Well, truthfully, she'd noticed it before when he was helping to load the bus, but this time she was up close and personal with them.

"Oh!" she gasped. "Was there a meeting or something that I forgot?"

He blinked then shook his head. "Oh, no! No. I…um…I wanted to talk to you."

"I'm not fired, am I?" It was a joke. Or at least half of one. Truthfully, she was nervous enough to welcome a firing.

He ran his hand through his hair and flushed. "God, no. Um, it'll just take…um…" He hesitated, looking into her room before flushing and looking down at the floor. Then he abruptly shoved his hands in his pockets. "So, would you like to take a walk?"

She exhaled. A walk sounded like a great idea. "I—"

"See, I'm going nuts like I always do before the first event. Paul is sick of me and threw me out of the room. We're sharing, you know. The others are down at the bar, but well, that just…" He huffed. "All those people make it worse. I'm sorry, you probably wanted some alone time. We've been stuck together on that bus for hours. I'm probably the last person you want to see."

She smiled at his rather morose expression. Clearly this man was on edge, even more than she was. "You always go nuts before an event?"

"No, no. Just the *first* event. After that, I'm too tired to get anxious."

She nodded. "So how many launches has your company done?"

"Like this with actors and a tour bus? Twice before. There were other little launches before that, but nothing on this scale. And nothing that makes me want to climb the walls like a chimpanzee on crack."

She laughed. He looked nothing like a chimpanzee, cracked or otherwise. "All right, monkey boy. I'm going to grab my shoes and I will be happy to walk wherever you want. Because I, too, am going a little nuts."

"Don't worry. You'll be great." It was an automatic response for him. She'd heard him say it to all the actors at one point or another in the past week. But she could also tell that he meant it.

Where he'd managed to find such confidence in her, she had no clue. But it was there, and it made her feel better. So she flashed him another smile then pulled on her shoes. Two minutes later, they were heading for the elevator.

"So where to, fearless leader?" she quipped.

He released a short laugh. "Didn't we just establish that I'm definitely not *fearless* tonight?"

She nodded as they got on the elevator and he punched the button for the lobby. "Okay, let me try again. What exactly are you worried about?"

He huffed. "There are a zillion things to worry about. The product launched nationally two days ago. If it flops, I could lose everything."

She swallowed. She'd forgotten that this was a make-or-break kind of deal for him. "I don't know how you do it, then. I'd be a nervous wreck."

"Mostly I bury myself in details. If you're focused on the little things, then it's hard to worry about the big things. Or at least harder. And we've already had some problems."

Her gaze snapped to his. "What? I mean, we have?"

He shrugged, but she could see the tension in the movement. "Not a big deal. Paul forgot some stuff, that's all."

"Important stuff?"

He sighed. "Yeah, important stuff, but I called my parents. They have a key to the office. Mom's overnighting some stuff to the hotel." He released a self-conscious laugh. "It's bad enough to call your mom for a rescue when you're twelve. At thirty, it's mortifying."

She laughed as the elevator finally arrived. "I doubt you do it often."

"Even so. Plus I hate the expense."

"I understand that. One time, we had this health fair at this hotel…" She regaled him with the story of her biggest show disaster. You couldn't do events without some sort of hiccup. By the time she was done, he was smiling and they were out of the hotel.

Fortunately, it was a balmy night in Texas. They were in a safe area right across from the comic-book shop where the event would be. They headed off toward the walkway that would lead to the nearby mall, walking in a comfortable silence. But at the corner, she turned to study his face. The lighting was harsh beneath a streetlight, so it picked out the furrows in his forehead, the slight hunch to his shoulders. Wow, he really was wound tight.

"So what set this off now? Why right before the first event?"

"Because there's nothing to do now. It's all done or in Tina and Paul's hands. But at the same time, it's also when the most things are unknown. I don't know how this group is going to mesh over the summer. I don't know if someone's going to be toxic or someone else is going to break a leg."

She laughed. "I think that's something actors say for good luck. 'Break a leg.' It's not going to happen."

"It did last year. The girl before Tina insisted on wearing ridiculous shoes even during teardown."

Ali laughed. "She didn't."

"She did on the second week. Tripped and snapped her ankle. We dropped her off at a hospital in New Jersey and had to leave her there the next morning."

"Okay, so you're good, then," she said. "You'd have to be

cursed or something for a broken leg to happen on two tours in a row."

He stopped dead in the center of the walk and groaned. "Do you know nothing about tempting the fates? You don't say things like that!"

She laughed because she knew it was a joke. "And here I thought you were a numbers guy, without a superstitious bone in your body."

"I *am* a numbers guy. But when there aren't numbers available, I'd fall back on praying to a voodoo priestess if I thought it would help."

She narrowed her eyes and looked around. "Sorry. I don't see any voodoo priestesses around. Maybe she has a kiosk in the mall."

He chuckled, the sound coming out lighter than before. "Good idea. We'll check there. But just in case she's closed, keep an eye out for a wishing well."

"Deal."

They walked in silence again, and Ali enjoyed the nice evening weather, the companionable walk to the mall, even the idea that there might be something fun to see inside the mall. And then about five feet away from the door, Ken completely destroyed her sense of peace.

"I also wanted to talk about that thing I said we didn't ever need to talk about."

8

KEN FELT READY TO jump out of his skin, but was trying to be mature. In truth, the last thing he wanted to do was discuss what they'd done in the parking garage. Not that he hadn't thought about it. It was practically *all* he thought about. All the tour worries were just distractions from his Ali obsession.

The problem was that he could see the same awareness in Ali's eyes every time they looked at each other. Ever since that night, her body did a kind of freeze whenever they ran into each other. It didn't last long, but it was there. Her shoulders tightened up. And once he thought she might have ducked around a corner to avoid talking to him. Sure, it could all be in his imagination, but he didn't think so.

Not that he blamed her, of course, but they couldn't continue the whole summer with her doing that. So he'd decided to confront her about it. Except right now she was being especially sweet, which made him think he'd imagined the whole thing.

"Oh," she said, obviously cringing. "Okay."

"I get the feeling that there's been some awkwardness between us. Not that I blame you or anything, but am I right?"

She licked her lips in nervousness, and his blood went straight south. Fortunately, she started talking so he hoped he was able to cover.

"I…well, yes, I suppose, but…" Her voice trailed away, and she looked distinctly uncomfortable.

"I'm so sorry, Ali. I didn't want— I shouldn't have…" He swallowed and forced himself to concentrate. "It was completely my fault. It won't ever happen again. I hope you won't leave the tour because of this. We really need you."

Her eyes widened, and then she squared her shoulders. A martial light entered her gaze and she abruptly grabbed his hand and pulled him away from the central mall entrance. Since this was an indoor/outdoor mall, she was able to lead them down a charming path that was currently empty of people.

"That's just it," she said when she finally slowed down. "I liked what we did. I like you. But you're my boss and this is weird, and I'm so sorry." Her last dozen words came out in a rush.

He knew he should say something, but his mind had completely stalled out on the fact that she liked him. Because he liked her. A lot.

"So…" she said and gestured to a restaurant/bar that was still open. "If we're going to keep talking about this, can we go into the bar?"

"You need some liquid courage?"

She flashed him her adorable smile that she half tried to hide. "No, I just like playing with the pink parasol."

"An umbrella-drink fan. I can work with that."

She rolled her eyes. "*Every* guy can work with that."

He paused a moment, wondering if there was an extra meaning in there. Was she thinking he was hitting on her? He wasn't. Not that he didn't want to. But…

He forcibly pulled his thoughts to a stop. She wasn't suggesting anything. She was just talking with him. Friend to friend…sort of.

"Uh, then we should go in," he tried.

She nodded. And then it was the awkward, you-first-no-you-first movement into the bar. How he longed to go back to the ease of just three minutes ago. But he'd started this— he could hardly complain when he'd been the one to make it awkward. Eventually, they worked it out and soon they were sitting at a table.

"Order whatever you like," he said. "My treat."

She smiled but then shook her head. "I think you're paying for enough," she said. "This one's on me." Then she leaned in. "You see, I've found this sweet deal for the summer. Costumes, makeup, parties all summer long. And I'm getting *paid* for it!"

"Wow," he drawled at her obvious joke. "What kind of sap does that?"

She smiled. "Only the best kind." Then the waitress appeared and she ordered a Malibu pineapple drink. He asked for a beer and nachos.

"Unless you want something else," he said, belatedly realizing that he should have asked if she wanted an appetizer.

"Nachos are great! Besides, aren't we leaving Texas tomorrow? Last stop before the food gets bland."

"A spicy girl, huh?"

"Within reason. I never saw the sense behind setting my mouth on fire just to prove my testosterone quotient."

"Brothers?" he asked.

"Boyfriend." She rolled her eyes. "I was definitely *not* impressed."

"Well, never fear with me. I promise to run screaming from any jalapeños."

"So you don't like spicy?"

"I love spicy if it's the right type." He flashed her a wink. It was not his best move. In fact, it wasn't his move at all, and in high school, he'd created a zillion of them. But with her, he found himself doing things on the fly without second-guessing himself so much. That was a good thing. Truthfully, it was a *great* thing. It wasn't that he was incredibly awkward around girls. But spending his past ten years buried in work had made his flirting skills extremely rusty.

Fortunately, she just laughed. Not so fortunately, the conversation stalled. The arrival of the drinks helped cover for a minute or so, but all too soon, he was sipping his beer and trying desperately to think of something cool to say. Thankfully, she stepped into the breech.

"My cousins really love Winning Guinevere."

"You played with them?"

"I took it over to their house a couple of days before I left. They told me I wasn't half bad for a girl."

"Ouch! Damned by faint praise."

She shook her head. "Not really. Their sister, my other cousin, is a tomboy and can kick her brothers' butts when it suits her. So I took it as a compliment whether they meant it that way or not."

He nodded. "Sounds like a wise choice."

"They said it's much better than your other game."

He grimaced. "Which one?"

"Leaper."

"Oh, yeah. That one bombed."

She started playing with her paper umbrella, spinning it in her fingers, opening it and closing it. He found himself fascinated by her fingers. Her hands were girl's hands, long, tapered fingers ending in sweetly contoured nails with fresh nail polish. She'd opted for a soft tone, a coral or something like that. Probably because it matched a costume. Tina was obsessive about details like that. He found he just liked it. Pretty, not bold, but with a shimmer that made him think of hidden depths.

"Did you throw a launch for that one?" she asked.

"Huh?"

"A launch like this for Leaper. Your game that—"

"Bombed. Right. No, that was early days. Before I figured

out that what I enjoyed in a game was not necessarily what the market wanted."

"So you liked Leaper?"

He nodded. "Loved it. Still play it sometimes."

"I'd like to try it."

He looked up and abruptly grinned. "Now you're just being nice." She opened her mouth to deny it, but he held up his hand. "Nope, you can't take it back now. You've promised to play it with me. After this launch is over. At the end of the summer, you and me, a Leaper party."

She smiled, and he watched those dimples appear again. "Agreed. I'll bring the nachos."

He groaned. "Hell, that means I'll have to find a blender to make…er, that."

She reached out and grabbed his beer to take a slug. "Nah. Beers are great." Then she pushed over her drink. "Here, you take the Malibu. I just wanted the umbrella."

He hated fruity drinks. Too much sweet, but he let her make the switch and drank every drop. And by the time it was gone, they were talking much more easily. They hit the normal topics—game design, bad marketing and bad girlfriend mistakes for him. Her topics were stupid health-fair customers, favorite college classes and bad boyfriend mistakes.

By the time they'd stuffed themselves on nachos and he'd finished another Malibu—she'd ordered it over his protests—they were laughing freely. He was coming to like fruity drinks, plus they could mock fence with the little umbrellas. Then the bar was closing—how late was it exactly?—and the two of them rushed giggling back to the hotel.

Honestly, it felt like a date with him walking her back to her room. Probably the best date of his life given that they were still laughing. That made it the most natural thing in the world to kiss her at the door, right? To press his mouth to hers, to lean against her body as he felt all its glorious hills and valleys. And she was kissing him back even as she opened her hotel-room door.

He hadn't meant to follow her inside. He really hadn't. But they kind of fell inside. He caught himself right before he toppled her to the floor. He wasn't that huge a guy, but she was definitely smaller than him. He didn't want to flatten her.

But she just kept going down to the floor, even when he tried to hold her up.

"You're too nice," she said as she dropped to her knees.

"You're too drunk," he shot back, even though he was laughing as he said it. "Come on, let's get you to bed."

"Hmmm," she said, shaking her head. "I'm not drunk after two beers."

"You had four."

"Did not!"

He frowned, trying to think. How much, exactly, had she had?

"That's what I keep thinking," she said. "You're too nice."

"I'm really not."

"You were in the garage," she said as she undid his belt buckle. He tried to jump backward, but he was trapped against the dresser.

"Ali!"

"And now it's time for you to get your turn."

He tried to stop her. He really did. But she was determined and within seconds, any blood in his brain rushed straight south. She was caressing him right through his pants. He was rock-hard, and at her first touch he nearly jumped onto the dresser. But there was no strength in his legs and what she did felt so good.

His jeans were unbuckled and pulled down in moments. He could have fought her. Hell, he *should* have fought her, but it had been a long time since he'd felt a woman there. His life had been his business for years now and…

Sweet heaven, he couldn't breathe. She'd already pushed

Living the Fantasy

down his clothes and now had him gripped in a hand with just the right tension.

"Ali," he groaned. "You don't—"

She took him in her mouth, all wet and hot and sure. That's what got him. She seemed so shy at times, but for something like this, she knew just what she wanted. And it was him! He'd braced his hands behind him to hold himself up. But now he reached a hand forward to touch her hair, to stroke her cheek.

"Ali," he tried again. "Don't. We shouldn't—"

She sucked him. Hard. And what she was doing with her tongue… He couldn't think. He was thrusting into her mouth, and he didn't intend to. This was so wrong.

"Oh, Ali," he breathed, feeling the charge build right behind his balls. His butt had gone tight, his legs were growing stronger, and his blood was beating to the pulse of her suction. But he couldn't do this. It wasn't right.

Reaching down, he grabbed her shoulders. He tried to be gentle, but everything in him was growing urgent. And if he didn't do this now, it would be too late.

"Ali!" he cried, as he forcibly pulled himself backward. He slid out—hell—but it was the right thing to do. "I can't let you do this." He said the words, but he didn't move himself out of her hand.

She didn't answer. She just looked up at him with a coy smile. God, she was beautiful. Not in a supermodel way, but in a mischievous, I-am-having-so-much-fun way. Which was a thousand times better. Her eyes sparkled and those dimples flashed. And then she did two things that undid him completely. First, she was smiling as she caught her lower lip—all flushed and red—in her teeth. And second, her thumb rubbed right below the ridge of his head.

Lightning washed his vision white and he surged forward toward her. He didn't want to release, but there was no stopping the rush and it was amazing. His whole body went into it. And his consciousness, too, because he was sure he blacked out for a moment.

But when he came back to himself it was to hear her giggling. He opened his eyes, horrible guilt washing through him. Then he saw her, and it just got worse. He'd released… over her.

"Oh, no," he breathed. "Oh, God. I'm sorry. I—"

"It's just a T-shirt!" she laughed as she pushed up from her knees. He scrambled to help her, but she was quick and graceful. A ton more coordinated than he was at the moment.

"Ali—"

She grinned at him, then ducked her head right before she disappeared into the bathroom. He was left standing there—or leaning there because his legs wouldn't support him—with his jeans at his ankles and his face burning. Worse, his brain kept spinning back and forth between what-have-I-just-done and can-we-do-that-again?

It took him a moment, but he forced himself to pull up his pants. He barely had the hand coordination to button himself when she came out, all smiling while her eyes danced with merriment.

He took a breath. "Ali, I…" He what? He had no freaking idea what he wanted to say.

And then, to his horror, she yawned. It was a tiny yawn, and one that she obviously fought. But one glance at the clock told him it was beyond late. Nearly 3:00 a.m.! Of course she was yawning. But talk about ego-crushing.

"Ali," he said, the words forming without conscious will. "That was amazing and I really enjoyed it. Though I'm sorry about your shirt."

She glanced down then shrugged, pulling it off with a quick tug. He didn't think he could get hard again so fast, but damn if his body didn't respond lightning-fast to her. Creamy skin, a red, lacy bra—red!—and then she dropped backward onto her bed with a whoosh, her arms completely spread open.

"God, I feel relaxed," she said.

She felt relaxed? The only solid part of his body right now was his growing boner.

"Ali, I want to climb into bed with you right now. I want it more than anything else," he said.

She rolled onto her side and flashed him a come-hither smile.

"I'm trying to be responsible here," he groaned. "You're drunk. *I'm* drunk. This is so not a good idea."

He watched as awareness entered her expression. It slipped in slowly. First her brows narrowed a bit, then her eyes widened. She blinked a few times before she seemed to realize she didn't have a shirt on. Her hand came up to cover her chest, and boy, did he mourn the loss of that sight.

He stepped forward, taking her hand in his. "Don't cover up. You're beautiful. And I'm a horrible boss who ought to be brought up on charges."

She shook her head. "No, no! This was all my idea!"

"Can I kiss you good-night, Ali? I really, really want to."

She shifted up onto her knees on the bed. Again, she was so graceful and her face was so beautiful. He just stood there and watched. Then he touched her face. It wasn't that he thought about what he was doing. He just started touching her. He caressed her cheek, he framed her jaw with his palm, and then he bent down to claim her lips.

Sweet. She was so sweet. And the lust was pounding through his body like a freight train. He took her lips and possessed her mouth. Then he nearly threw her to the bed and did what any caveman would.

But he couldn't. He was her boss and he'd started this evening trying to make up for what he'd done with her in the parking garage.

It was the hardest thing he'd had to do ever, but he ended the kiss. He pulled back, he touched her face, he stole a look at her gorgeous breasts even though he shouldn't. And then he forced himself to back away.

"Thank you, Ali Flores."

"For what?" she quipped. "I was just returning the favor."

He had no answer, but apparently one came to his lips anyway. "Thank you for being you." Then he backed out of her room.

ALI HEARD THE DOOR TO HER ROOM click shut and dropped backward onto the bed with a whump. She wasn't nearly as drunk as she'd pretended. That was her dirty secret. Tomorrow she'd have the excuse ready—oh my, I was totally smashed when we did that—but tonight, she couldn't lie to herself. She'd wanted him to make love to her. And she'd wanted to drive him wild with a blow job.

She'd obviously succeeded with the second. The first had been stopped by his honor. Hell, who'd have thought that she'd be annoyed by any guy's sense of honor!

On some level, she knew he was right. She wasn't thinking exactly clearly right now. But they'd had so much fun this evening. She hadn't laughed that hard in years. They'd even played a mock sword fight with their umbrellas! He was a great guy and she wanted to have hot sex with him.

That was the bold, honest truth. And now she had to respect his sense of honor—sigh—and climb alone into her cold hotel bed. If she was a good, wholesome, honest person, she wouldn't tempt him again all summer.

She giggled as she pressed her face into her pillow. Guess she wasn't a good, wholesome or honest person. Who knew?

9

ALI WASN'T NERVOUS before going on stage. No, she was more of the get-sick-and-pass-out variety of panicked. She hyperventilated. She had sweaty palms. And nothing anyone said to her made it any better.

She'd been thinking of this summer as basic booth work. It was, except for the "show" part. The wedding between Arthur and Guinevere was on a *stage,* and her one middle-school experience with being on stage had been a disaster. That had been over ten years ago, but she still remembered walking to the center and forgetting every line.

"Wow, do you look good in that outfit or what?"

Ali turned to see Ken smiling at her. He was looking regal in his King Arthur getup. Tunic, belt, boots and a robe that swept the floor as he walked. Once again she noticed muscle definition, this time in his legs. Nice! And quite the distraction from her current difficulties.

"Nice costume," she managed to say.

"No one's going to be looking at me."

Ali looked down. Silk sheath, corset about to burst and classy-looking half boots. She did look sexy. She even *felt* sexy, which was awesome. Normally that would be a great thing, except that it was somewhat hard to breathe *and* be sexy. It had taken two of the girls to tie her into this thing, and she seriously doubted that any blood flow was going up to her brain.

Normally she would take a deep breath to calm her nerves, but that wasn't going to happen. The best she could do was stand tall and breathe into her upper lungs. Which naturally lifted her chest a little higher. Which the guys seemed to appreciate. She just hadn't realized how constricting it was to look sexy.

"Um, thanks," she said. Normally a heartfelt compliment like that would have bolstered her confidence. It did make her smile, but one look out at the audience had her breaking into panic.

The "small comic-book shop" was actually pretty big because they didn't do anything small in Texas. What no one had told her was that they had shifted the event to the main mall stage. At the moment, there were a few hundred people in the audience, and a few thousand more shopping.

"Tell me again why I thought this was a good idea," she said.

"Because it's fun."

She shot him an incredulous look, and he just laughed.

"Trust me, Ali. You're going to be great. Just be yourself." Then he peeked through the curtains at the crowd. "And don't forget to look longingly at Blake."

She grimaced. Blake was Lancelot, and yes, he sure did look pretty. But she didn't want to look at him. She wanted to stay with Ken. Preferably in another state and far away from any crowd.

"Ali—" Ken began, but at that exact moment, the music started. Standing in the wings, they got to watch as Samantha, the tavern wench, came on stage and started talking about the royal wedding. Paul bantered back as Mordred with snide comments appropriate to the villain of the piece.

The crowd got into it, especially as Blake started wandering through as Lancelot. He, too, got to make some witty remarks. Most of it was unscripted, and all of it was fun. Which made Ali abruptly realize how sunk she was. Extemporaneous banter? She sucked at that!

"I can't do this," she said, her heart sinking.

"Not a problem," Ken answered as he gently dropped a hand on her shoulder. "I don't want you to do what they're doing."

She glanced at him. "Yes, you do. You want me to work the crowd, to get them excited about the game, to—"

"I want you to be you. Stand on stage and smile. Say your lines and when it's time, step down into the crowd and just talk to them."

"But—"

"Ali, you can do this."

It was almost time for them to go on stage. She could hear the steady march of the mini-play behind her. But Ken didn't let her look out there anymore. Instead, he turned her to face him.

"One more thing, Ali," he said.

"What?"

"To the day I die, I will always regret walking out of your room last night." Then he kissed her. Deep and full on her mouth.

It was obviously a ploy and it shouldn't have worked. But it did. After all, she'd been aching for his kiss forever. And just because it came now, right before she was going on stage, did nothing to take away from the power of being pressed up against his body again. Of feeling his tongue sweep in and possess her in a very elemental way. She opened for him, she melted into him, she did everything but strip him naked and take him to her bed. And then, damn him, he slowly pulled away.

"Until my dying day," he murmured. Then he grabbed her arm and shoved her onto the stage. She barely had time to recover her balance. No time at all to regain any sense of equilibrium. But that was okay because her first line was about how difficult it was to marry a stranger. According to legend, she and Arthur had never met before their wedding day.

Ashley sauntered up as Morgan le Fey. She was the female baddie, and she played the part to perfection. Guinevere was supposed to be young and naive at this point, so it was right in character when it took Ali two tries to get her words out. But she was able to do it, and soon she was settling into her role as she crossed to center stage. Except it wasn't so easy to walk in three-inch heels and there was an irregularity in the stage. Ali's heel caught and she nearly went down to the floor in an inglorious heap. Fortunately, she saw a young man start to jump up from his seat as if to catch her.

"Do you think you could help me?" Ali asked, her voice rather breathy. She didn't know if it came from just being kissed or from the fact that she was still wobbly, but apparently the boy heard. He was out of his seat and on stage in a flash.

The kid was about fifteen years old, gangly and with unfortunate acne. But he had a nice smile that she responded to. He took her hand and helped her walk down the stage.

"You're so kind," she said.

"Don't worry," he said. "I've got you."

She smiled her thanks. "Yes," she said, "you do. Thank you. You are very strong." She said it because it was true. He had a solid grip on her arm, and she was less afraid of falling.

Apparently, it was the perfect thing to say. He flushed a hot red and suddenly became her most devoted follower. He escorted her to her place on the stage. She spoke her lines and interacted with the other actors. And all the while, the boy stood right by her side, apparently very proud of his new position. A discreet glance at the crowd told her that a few of them were looking enviously at the young man, especially as she knighted him, giving him the name Sir Gary.

And at that moment, Blake must have realized he was

being upstaged. As Lancelot, he should be the one at her side. So he made a dashing leap onto the stage, introduced himself and then offered her his arm. Poor Gary was ready to retreat, but Ali would have none of that. She kept both "knights" by her side.

And then Ken came on stage. Or rather, it was King Arthur in full royal regalia. His voice boomed across the mall as he welcomed everyone to his wedding. He was every inch a king, and Ali couldn't help but stare. He was magnificent!

So when he held out his hand to her, she completely forgot Lancelot and Gary. She stepped straight up to Ken just like the queen she was supposed to be. Then together they turned and were "married" by Merlin, who was played by the owner of the comic-book shop.

Her lines were simple. All she had to say was "I do." But at that moment, holding on to Ken's hand and looking into his eyes, she had a flash of a real wedding. Of saying yes to marriage with this man who had made her laugh so hard last night. Who had given her a memory of ecstasy in a parking garage. It was ridiculous, and so very inappropriate, but she couldn't stop herself from thinking about it. From feeling it.

And then she said, "I do" as if she really did.

She saw his eyes widen in surprise, then darken with some sort of emotion. She didn't dare try to interpret it, but his hands were shaking as he lifted her crown. Guinevere didn't get a ring. Instead, she knelt before Ken and let him crown her.

She was supposed to look to Lancelot then. They were setting up a love triangle, after all. But she didn't want to. She wanted to straighten up and kiss her king as if they were gloriously in love. But she was *acting,* she reminded herself, so she forced herself to look sideways at Blake. Funny how she'd once thought him incredibly handsome. Right then, she wondered how the man was going to compete with the very regal Ken.

Then the show was over. Ken clapped his hands and invited all his guests to partake of refreshments and play the game that was set up on monitors all around the central mall area. Paul, too, stepped up and called, "Let the games begin!"

Within moments, a full third of the audience was organized around monitors, beginning the game play. The rest gathered around card tables to start with the tabletop play. Or at least pre-video play. It wasn't necessary to the game, but it could add an extra dimension. Plus, it kept people busy while others were using the electronics.

Seeming reluctant to leave, Sir Gary stayed by her side, handing out game pages, helping to explain the rules. He even spent a few moments entertaining an unruly toddler while an older sibling got time to play.

Lord, she didn't know how she'd managed to pick the one boy out of the audience who was a gem, but she had. She made sure to keep his duties light, and within about forty-five minutes, Tina showed up to escort both her and Gary back to the stage where the really large view screen was up.

"My, aren't you a lucky one," Tina cooed in her best tavern-wench voice. "Assisting our queen."

"It wasn't anything," Gary hedged.

"It was a very great deal," Ali responded. "And for your help, you shall now have a very great reward." She prayed she wasn't lying.

"Nay, Sir Gary Stevens," cut in Paul/Mordred in his booming voice. "Do you think it is an easy thing to win a queen's favor?"

"Er…" Gary began. "I, uh…"

"You must prove yourself worthy. You must show us on the field of battle! Are you prepared?"

Gary looked anxiously behind him at the audience. "Um, I haven't gotten to play at all. I don't know—"

"Then it shall be a true test of skill and cunning."

"Don't worry," Ali put in, squeezing his arm. "I believe in you."

Gary flushed and nodded, taking the game controller in his hand.

Paul grinned. "Then we shall begin."

And so, just as the audience had started to get bored, Paul and Gary caught their attention yet again as "Sir Gary" began his quest on the big screen.

It was fun to watch, especially with Paul and Tina making all sorts of wry comments. And when those two grew tired, Samantha stepped in and kept the audience in stitches by camping it up with Lancelot. Meanwhile, Ali slipped off the stage and continued to work the tables, helping where she could. Chatting when she couldn't.

Basic booth work. The idea was to keep the people happy and hanging around long enough that they finally ended up buying the product. Which, by the way, was selling at a very steady clip.

It turned out it was easy. She wasn't talking about blood-pressure medicines or cholesterol pills like at her old job. No, this time she got to talk games and books with a crowd of kids. Truthfully, she didn't understand half of what they said, but she knew enough to smile and laugh when it was called for.

It took about twenty minutes, but she realized that most of the kids didn't care that she didn't understand what they said. What mattered was that she listened. And she did, or at least she tried to. With what felt like hundreds of kids, it was hard to tell if she got anywhere with any of them. She did know that the time flew by. Six hours. Six hours! And it felt like ten minutes. Except for the fact that she was exhausted by the end and still the kids seemed to linger beside her, wanting to talk.

She worked with them patiently. Behind her, Tina, Paul and Ken were tearing down the equipment. The actors were laughing, pitching in with the work while congratulating each other on an event well done. But Ali was still with the remaining kids. And Gary. Faithful Gary who was flushed and happy from a successful campaign on the big screen.

She was beginning to feel the strain, wondering if she could keep it up much longer, when Ken appeared by her side.

"I'm so sorry," he said to the remaining seven holdouts. "I'm afraid my lady Guinevere needs to return to her duties. No rest for my queen."

The kids laughed at that, but not mockingly. They seemed to truly be happy to let her stay in character even when breaking off.

"But," continued Ken, "I'd like to hand you these coupons. They're a really good deal. Give them to your friends. Mail them to your cousins—"

"Give them to your girlfriends' brothers," Ali added, "so they won't interrupt your dates."

All the kids giggled at that. They were all too young to have a girlfriend, but that didn't mean they weren't blissfully imagining it.

"And," continued Ken, "if you have a gaming club or just a big group of friends, my email address is on there. Email me and we'll hook you up."

Thanks and appreciative murmurs went around as they all took the coupons.

"Don't thank me," answered Ken. "Thank Queen Guinevere."

They did. Every single one of them smiled at her and in all seriousness, thanked her with grave voices. She accepted their appreciation as regally as possible.

Then, just like that, the event was over. Ken took her hand and led her away. Behind her, the others were wheeling out the carts, and it almost looked like an entourage was following her out the door.

Amazing. Incredible. Ali couldn't believe it was done or

that it had been so...well, not exactly easy, but fun. It had been fun!

So why, in all of this, were her only thoughts about Ken, his kiss and the words *I do?*

10

ALI WAS ASLEEP, curled up like a kitten in her bus seat. Ken had taken the seat across the aisle from her, hoping to find a moment to talk with her. But whereas everyone else on the bus was still high on the success of the event, Ali was an introvert. She could be spectacular in a crowd—and she had been—but at the end of the event, she was exhausted. Which meant that, unlike the extroverts who were chattering away toward the back, Ali was out, and Ken—who hovered between exhausted and exhilarated—sat a seat away and just watched her.

He'd never been so amazed by a person before. She'd made him laugh last night until his sides ached. She'd been terrified just before going on stage, but she'd come through just like the queen she was. She'd charmed everyone, himself included, and he was halfway in love with her. It didn't hurt that she revved his engine like no one else, too.

He couldn't stop thinking about the moment they'd said their pretend "I do." He knew it was pretend. He knew they were acting, but it had felt so real. She had been so beautiful and he had wanted to marry her. He'd wanted her to be his queen with a hunger that both stunned and terrified him.

He might have done something stupid then. He might have hauled her up and kissed her. But at that moment, she'd

turned slightly and looked at Blake/Lancelot. That had been
the bucket of cold water he'd needed. She was *acting,* for
God's sake. And only a fool would take it as anything but
pretend. But for those few short moments, he had felt like a
real king with Ali as his queen.

He leaned back in his seat, letting his own eyelids grow
heavy. This was either going to be the worst or the best summer of his life.

HE WAS KEEPING AN EYE ON HER. Ali was dead on her feet—or
on her butt since she was sitting in the bus seat—but there
was a simmering excitement in her blood that kept her from
falling completely unconscious. Part of it was the certain
knowledge that Ken was sitting right across the bus aisle from
her just watching her as she pretended to sleep.

It should have felt weird. Instead, it felt exciting. Arous-
ing. She could easily fantasize that she was curled up on a
couch in her apartment while someone hot and exciting was
standing guard outside. It wasn't like he was a Peeping Tom.
In her mind, he was just like Ken—sweet and funny—only
like a P.I. sent to protect her.

Because of his job, he'd be forced to look on as she slowly
stretched on her couch then piece by piece, peeled off her
clothes because it was so hot inside her apartment. And while
Ken would be fighting the urge to burst through the door
and take her right there on her living-room rug, she would
be doing an unconscious striptease for him. Or maybe not
so unconscious because maybe she knew he was there and
wanted him to burst in.

She felt her nipples tighten and her core go hot and liquid. And that was really frustrating because she was on a
bus with a half dozen other people. She wanted it to be just
her and Ken.

Lord, when would she learn that she should *not* fantasize

about her boss? But she couldn't stop herself, and so, as the miles slipped by, she let her mind drift into some very pleasant places.

THEIR NEXT STOP WAS an amusement park where they would be for the next ten days. Their job was to do a show on the main stage once a day, and then draw people to their booth throughout the rest of the park hours. Which meant that, for the most part, Ali got up at eight, grabbed some breakfast, then put on her costume. They worked in shifts until the park closed at eleven at night with time off throughout the day to eat junk food and sneak in a roller-coaster ride or three. She then collapsed into bed at midnight or later, only to do it all again the next day.

It was grueling. The weather was hot, and though the booth had air-conditioning for the electronics, she was supposed to be outside in the crowd drawing people into the booth. So she stood in the sun in a leather corset and was very grateful to be wearing a silk shift underneath.

At least she didn't have the sunburn problem that her fairer coworkers had. Samantha, the redhead, was using industrial-strength sunscreen by the bucketful. Even Ashley, as the brunette Morgan le Fey, claimed she'd just come from a fight with a dragon who'd nearly burned her to a crisp.

She barely saw Ken, more's the pity. He was there, of course, but always working. The main stage show was supposed to reveal the rising attraction between herself and Lancelot. There were all sorts of feats of manly combat and suggestive flirtations. Truthfully, the only fun part for her was when Ken hit the stage as King Arthur. She knew she was supposed to be attracted to Lancelot, but she only had eyes for her king, especially the few times he strapped on a sword and started mock fighting. There was something about a guy with a sword that just turned her on.

But as soon as the stage event was finished, they were

right back at the booth selling the game. In short, the team used this time to settle into a rhythm. The main show became a well-oiled machine. The group all became friends, some closer than others. And Ali felt that her relationship with Ken was becoming entrenched in friendly camaraderie. Very nice, but it just made her nighttime fantasies all the more heated.

And then came the *hot* day. Not just hot, but a blistering 104 degrees. Everyone was cranky except for Paul. The VP of marketing loved it because where else would the public go when it was that hot but inside an air-conditioned booth? They were crammed to the gills every minute and sales were through the roof.

Meanwhile, Ken declared that no one could be outside for more than twenty minutes at a time. And Ali thought if she spent two more minutes listening to the stuttering of another prepubescent boy or smiled at one more tired mother with a cranky kid, her brains would boil. Literally boil right out of her ears.

She was about three seconds from losing it when Ken grabbed her arm and pulled her to a tiny alcove to the side of the booth.

"Oh my God, I'm going to explode." That was him speaking, and he'd taken the words right out of her mouth.

"My shift doesn't end for another ten minutes," she whispered. It wasn't quite 5:00 p.m., but she was counting the seconds until she could leave.

"You started a half hour early because Blake started throwing donuts at Samantha and I tossed them both out. So I declare your shift done. Mine, too."

She chuckled as he aimed her straight for a park exit. "I didn't realize the boss had a shift."

"Of course I do. It's the work-until-you're-going-to-kill-someone shift. And I just hit my limit."

"About damn time," she murmured as she climbed into the van. It was one of those ubiquitous white metal things and it usually hauled around the electronics. But everything was in the booth now, so what was behind them was an eerily empty stack of shelving units and snakes of cables piled into the corner.

Ken was a step behind her, hopping into the driver's seat.

"So where we going, boss?" she asked as she aimed the air vents straight at her overheated face.

"Name your favorite place to detox."

"A library."

He paused a moment. "Seriously?"

She shrugged. "You don't actually have to study in a library, you know. People always assume you are, but you can do just about anything so long as you're quiet."

His expression shifted into a slow smile. "Anything?"

She grinned, her mind going right where it always did when she had a moment with Ken—straight into the X-rated territory. "Just about."

"But I don't know any libraries around here."

"Good because what I really want is a swimming pool."

"God, yes. You read my mind." He immediately put the van in gear.

She sighed as the air-conditioning began to take hold. "Yeah, that would be lovely, except that there will be a zillion kids at the pool."

He nodded. "Yeah, maybe at our hotel. But you forget, I've done this summer trip twice before."

She rolled her head to look at him. "Yeah?"

He grinned. "Yeah. I'm also someone who understands about hotel chains and frequent user points."

Her eyebrows lifted. "Any hotel pool is going to be buried in kids right now."

"Trust me?"

"I do." She said it without hesitation, but his expression shifted.

"Ali…" That was it. Just her name, but she heard a wealth

of meaning underneath it. And it told her without words that he had been tortured by some of the same thoughts and feelings that she had. That he wanted something he shouldn't— not as her boss—and that this was a chance for them to express it to each other. Appropriate or not, he wanted to explore.

And so did she.

So she touched his arm. And then she got bolder and stroked her fingers down his forearm to touch his fingers where they were on the steering wheel.

"I trust you, Ken." *And I want you.* She didn't say the last part out loud, but maybe her eyes did. Maybe something in her words tipped him off because she saw his eyes darken and his nostrils flare. Then he took the freeway with a little extra gusto.

Twenty minutes later and they were walking into a cool lobby with very smartly dressed people standing behind dark mahogany counters. They didn't even blink at the way she was dressed. They simply smiled and asked if there was anything they could do to help.

"Is the presidential suite available?" Ken asked.

"One moment, sir," said the young man behind the counter as he typed on his keyboard. "Yes, it is."

Ken passed over his ID. "I believe I have enough points to have it for one night."

Again, nothing but a smooth smile as the man typed. Five minutes later and they were on their way up to the twenty-seventh floor with special gold keycards in their sweaty grips.

"You know what he was thinking," Ali said as they stood side by side in the elevator. The man probably thought she was a hooker, purchased for the afternoon. If it weren't so mortifying, she might have laughed at the situation.

"I don't care what he thinks," Ken all but growled. "So long as room service and the air-conditioning work, he can think anything he wants."

"Easy for you to say. You're not the one traipsing about in a corset and half boots." And if this wasn't the most bizarre hooker gear, she didn't know what would be.

He grimaced, obviously feeling remorse for his words. "You don't look anything like a hooker, Ali."

She arched her brows at him. "Doesn't matter—"

"And your face is too sweet to be mistaken for one."

She frowned, unsure whether to be insulted or complimented. No, she didn't want to look like a prostitute. But she didn't want to be thought of as so sweet that no one had lustful thoughts when they looked at her. She wasn't a nun.

"And besides," he added, "I'm in costume, too."

Barely. As boss, he got the most minimal of costumes. His kingly gear was in his cape and crown. Once he ditched that, he walked around in leather pants and an old cotton shirt. In some places, he might have passed as trendy. Thankfully, there wasn't time for her to answer as the elevator dinged. There wasn't even a hallway. The doors just opened onto a suite that was larger than her apartment. Cool air enveloped her so fast and so quickly that she sneezed. But that did not detract from what she was looking at.

A kitchenette, a living room, a bedroom and a balcony with… "It's got its own pool. Holy crap! There's a pool out there on the balcony."

"It's just a little one."

True. It was just a little kidney-shaped thing. But it was completely private because it was blocked on all sides by greenery.

"This isn't the presidential suite," she murmured. "This is the movie-star suite complete with ways to block telephoto lenses from the paparazzi!" She spun back to Ken. "Just how many frequent user points did you spend?"

He shrugged. "All of them." He joined her at the sliding door to the balcony. "I stayed here for a conference once."

"Here as in the hotel, or here as in up *here* with the kitchen and the pool and probably your own towel girl."

He laughed. "No towel girl, I swear. But yeah, they messed up my reservation and I ended up here."

"Lucky you!"

He shook his head. "That's just it. I kept thinking, what a waste! I worked the whole time and was never even here. All I did was sleep and grab an espresso on the way out the door."

"An espresso?"

He gestured to the kitchen counter where there was indeed a machine for espresso shots. "It only took me three tries to figure it out."

She laughed—a real carefree, relaxed laugh—for the first time in days. She was cool, standing in the lap of luxury, and alone with Ken. What more could a girl want? Except... "Oh, hell. I don't have a bathing suit."

"Sure you do." He stepped over to a closet and swung the doors open. There, folded neatly on one of the shelves, was a small variety of bathing suits from men's swim trunks to bikinis, with various one-piece suits thrown in. "Loaners. They're cleaned after every use."

"Oh my God. I've stepped into a Hollywood movie and didn't even notice."

He grinned. "Only the best for my queen." And then he sobered. "Look, I don't know about you, but I've been dreaming of that pool since the minute the thermometer hit sweltering. So I'm going to shower and change and submerge."

"Rock-paper-scissors-lizard-Spock for first use of the shower."

His eyebrows rose. "Wow, where did you learn that?"

"Paul taught me. We were fighting over the last pineapple slice." She held up her fist in the traditional rock-paper-scissors stance, all the while grinning because she'd surprised him with her geek know-how.

Meanwhile, he frowned in mock outrage. "Hey, those were my points that paid for this room!"

"And yet chivalry demands that you let the lady go first."

"Oh, my damnable honor!"

She raised her fist a little higher. "This is the only way to assuage both your honor and give you a fighting chance at being the first in the pool."

He grimaced but held up his fist. "Okay, but I warn you. I don't always pick Spock."

"Good to know," she said in mock seriousness. She didn't really care who showered first. There was plenty of time for both of them, but this made it fun. And she liked that she could banter with him like that.

They pumped fists and she won. He had indeed picked Spock. She'd correctly guessed that his earlier comment was a way to throw her off, so she'd gone with lizard, which poisons Spock. Which meant after a gleeful chortle, she danced happily into the bathroom. "I'll be quick!"

"That's what they all say!"

She laughed and switched on the light, only to gasp in stunned delight. The bathroom was roughly the same size as the bus. Or at least it felt that way. Whirlpool bath, extra-large shower, double-sink counter, not to mention a separate makeup area. She opened a closet looking for linens only to discover that there was a separate room for the commode.

Now she really did feel like a queen. Or at least a princess. Mindful of her promise to be quick, she started to undress. Or rather, she planned to, until she realized she was in a corset that tied in the back.

Oh, hell.

"Um, Ken?" She popped open the door and peeked out. "Ken?"

He looked up from where he sat at the conveniently provided hotel computer. "Yeah?"

"I need some help here." She stepped out and gestured behind her back. "Without help, I'm stuck in this thing."

"Oh, right. No problem."

He straightened up from the desk, and she stared at him as the pieces started falling into place in her head. So far this trip, she'd seen him working constantly at the booth helping to make sales or hunched over his computer. Except for their very memorable night before the mall event, he hadn't done anything else but those two things.

And now she was two minutes in the bathroom, and he was already on the computer. "Either you're a workaholic, or you're worried about something," she said.

"Workaholic," he said without missing a beat.

She shook her head. "I don't think so."

He gestured for her to turn around. "No, really. Definitely a workaholic."

She didn't move an inch. "No, my boss at the hospital is a workaholic. He's always at work and when he's not there, he's talking work. At lunch, at parties, on weekends when he's supposed to be with his kids, it's all jabber jabber jabber. Hospital this, publicity that, event extravaganza whatever."

He frowned. "How would you know that? You spend time at parties and weekends with your boss?"

"Sure. I remember one hospital-sponsored community event. I was there working. He was there with his kids."

"And?"

"And, he had his smartphone going all the time. Barely even looked up when his kid went to bat in the softball game."

Ken pursed his lips. "Well, I don't have kids but—"

"You don't exist with a phone plastered to your ear and an iPad on your lap."

He grimaced. "Yeah, I do."

"Lately, maybe. Because you're worried about something. And I'll bet if you had a chance to see your kid play softball, you wouldn't even have a phone with you."

"I always carry my phone."

"Really?" She looked at his belt where it was usually strapped. Not there.

He patted his belt, then cursed. "I must have left it in the van."

"Ding ding! I win!" she crowed.

"Because I forgot my phone?"

She nodded. "Because workaholics would never forget their phones and would be panicked if they did—"

"I am panicked!"

"You're irritated at yourself. But you're going to get over it and leave it in the van because I have mine." She pointed to the corner where she'd dropped her purse.

"I doubt we'd get the same kind of calls."

"No, but anyone who desperately needs to contact you will think to call me when they can't find you." She frowned, wondering if he could follow those confused words. "And now before you completely distract me, you're going to tell me what's the problem."

"There is no problem."

"Then you wouldn't have desperately needed this escape. You don't mind the crowds like I do."

He frowned. "The crowds bother you?"

"We're not talking about me!" she huffed. "And it's not so bad. But they do get exhausting."

He nodded. "I hear that."

"And I want to hear what the problem is," she said sternly. One month ago, she wouldn't have pushed so hard. After all, he was right: this was his company, not hers. But something about playing a queen on stage had gotten into her. She felt more assertive than ever before. It was as if she'd been forced to confront her shyness. After two weeks of playing Guinevere, standing up on stage no longer frightened her. And standing up to Ken seemed like child's play. So she dropped her hands on her hips and took a stab in the dark. "The release of the game was last week. I thought we were doing well."

"Our events are doing fine. Great, actually. But nationwide figures are…well, it's too early to count." He lifted his shoulder in a defensive gesture that she recognized from her own mirror. He was putting on a brave face, but inside he was worried as hell.

"How bad are the early indications?"

He shook his head. "Not that bad. And besides, it's not your problem. All you have to do is be my queen."

She snorted. "Well, this queen is also your friend. And as your friend, I want you to talk to me. What's the problem?"

He waited a long moment. She thought at first that he wasn't going to confess. But in the end, the weight of it all got him talking. His shoulders slumped, his hands slid down the sides of his pants as if he was looking for pockets and, most telltale of all, his gaze dropped to the floor.

"It's not so bad. There are sales. But, you know, they're about on par with Leaper."

"Leaper? The product that *flopped?*"

He winced and she immediately regretted her harsh word. "Like I said, it's early still. It's not like I get real-time sales reports."

"But there's a downloadable version, right? Not as complicated or as good as the big-deal one. But it's like a teaser to lure you into the more expensive version."

He nodded and didn't speak. So she prodded him.

"And those are the sales numbers you have been watching. Because you can see those in real time."

Again he nodded but kept his lips buttoned.

"Oh, hell, they're bad, aren't they?"

He sighed. "I think I need some beer. What about you? Or would you prefer another Malibu pineapple thing?"

She watched as he pulled out the room-service menu, seeing it for the avoidance tactic it was. Worse, it was avoiding via booze. Translation: sales were really bad.

Ah, hell!

11

KEN STUDIED THE ROOM-SERVICE MENU as if he was prepping for a final exam. He didn't want to talk about the dismal sales reports or what they might mean to his company. Talking about a disaster didn't help avoid it. Or wouldn't in this case. All he wanted to do was drink, eat and have sex. Not necessarily in that order.

"So," Ali said as she stepped right up to him. She was still in her corset, still looking like the queen he'd envisioned since…well, since he was a child. Not the actual look or costume. As always, the looks were secondary to what he felt around her: warmth, compassion, humor and a whole lot of sexy.

"I'll order dinner," he said. "What would you like?"

She touched his arm, and when he steadfastly refused to look at her, she touched his face. No way he could refuse her now. So he turned and looked right into her very beautiful eyes.

"First, Ken, answer one question. Is there anything we can do now to help sales? Beyond what we're already doing?"

He shook his head. If there was, he'd already be doing it.

"You and Paul have been over this a zillion times, haven't you?"

"I have. Paul's been…" He shook his head. "Paul's been distracted lately."

She frowned. "By what?"

"I wish I knew." And what a time for his VP of marketing to suddenly flake out on him. It wasn't anything overt, but the man just seemed half there at times. Paul went through the motions, but his mind was obviously somewhere else. Meanwhile, Ali had been doing some thinking on her own.

"First things first," she said as she turned off the computer.

"Hey!"

"You don't need to be looking at that. You need to be ordering dinner and thinking of ways to relax." She started flipping through the room-service menu. "What are you having?"

"Lasagna." It was his go-to meal when traveling anywhere.

She nodded. "Good choice. I'll have the spinach salad—"

He rolled his eyes. "You don't have to diet—"

"And the black silk pie." She flashed him a grin. "Why eat a meal when you can make one out of dessert?"

"Healthy and sinful. I like it."

"I think you should get the cheesecake. I mean, if you like cheesecake."

"What about the hot lava cake?"

She pursed her lips. "I can work with that, although that is two chocolate desserts."

"Hmmm, good point. Does that mean we're going to share desserts?"

She grinned. "I will if you will."

"Oh, I will. I more than will." He blinked. Had that made any sense at all? It was a small thing, but he loved the intimacy of sharing food with a woman. It was something he only did with a girlfriend. And though Ali wasn't at that status yet, he wanted her to be. And so he wanted to share desserts with a freakish kind of want.

She chuckled. "So I guess you'll have to decide what you're going to order."

He grinned and picked up the phone. He ordered beer—she didn't want the fruity thing—salad and lasagna, then all three desserts.

"Ooo!" she cooed. "I like how you think!"

He hung up the phone. "And I'd like to get you out of that corset now."

She blinked at him. "Wow, going for the gusto there."

He flushed. He hadn't exactly meant it as a come-on. Mild flirtation, certainly, but—

She burst out laughing. "Relax, Ken. I know you were teasing." She turned around. "And yes, please loosen this. I would really like to breathe again."

He went straight for her ties in back. After two other launches like this one, he was an expert at tying—and un-tying—corsets. But as he started tugging the knot apart, he couldn't resist looking at the smooth curve of her neck or the beautiful latte color of her skin. If she were his girlfriend, he would be kissing her neck right now. As he loosened the corset and pushed it down, he would nuzzle the shift open, as well. Eventually, both corset and shift would drop to the ground and he would wrap his arms around her. He'd slip his hands across her shoulders, down her arms, until he could slide in and cup her breasts. He would do it slowly, sweetly, and she would melt backward into his arms.

She took a deep breath, and from this angle, he could see the lift and lower of her breasts.

"God, it's good to breathe."

He nodded, even though she couldn't see it. He liked see-ing her body move as the restriction on her torso eased. All women did it. They took a deep breath then kind of wiggled inside their corset. They stretched on each side and always sighed in delight as their body was freed. He watched Ali go through those exact motions, appreciating every second of the display.

"I gotta say, my back never felt so good," Ali commented.

"Usually after days on my feet, my whole body aches. With a corset, it's just my feet that burn by day's end."

"I promise to rub your feet after dinner."

"You *are* my hero!"

"But only if you promise to watch a movie with me while I do it."

She tilted her head. "What movie?"

He grabbed the guide and flipped through it. "*Terminator 3? Blade Runner,* director's cut?"

She choked back a laugh. She had a hand on her belly, holding the corset in place as she turned around to look at the guide. "Sci-fi action fan?"

"We could try *Space Balls*. That's sci-fi spoof."

"Yeah, it was too much to hope for a foot rub *and* a romantic comedy."

He mock rolled his eyes. "Way too much."

"Fine. How about…?"

They set about negotiating movie choices. She liked romantic comedy and mystery with a paranormal twist. He went for the science fiction that wasn't kid stuff and anime. In the end they agreed on the TV pilot of *Terra Nova*. Neither of them had seen it, but it had enough elements for them both to be happy.

"But first," she said firmly, "I need a shower."

"Yeah," he pretend-groused. "You said you'd be done like ten minutes ago."

She stuck out her tongue at him, a gesture that immediately sent his blood straight south, and then disappeared into the bathroom with a laugh. He sighed and dropped back down into the desk chair. He was just reaching for the computer when she called from the bathroom.

"And if you touch that computer while I'm in here, then I'm going to make you watch a Jennifer Aniston movie!"

He pulled his hand back with a snap. "That's so not

fair! What am I going to do while you're luxuriating in the shower?"

"Suffer!" she called right before the shower started.

He was suffering, he thought as he adjusted his pants. But it was a good kind of pain.

ALI SHOWERED QUICKLY, and boy, was it great to clean the dust and grime away. Then she put on one of the very lush hotel robes and stepped out. Ken was waiting right where she'd left him—next to the computer with a strange expression on his face. Kind of happy, kind of in pain.

"Were you on the computer?"

"Nope."

"What were you doing?"

"Thinking."

"Work thinking?"

"Nope."

She looked at him, at the slight smirk on his face and the way his arms covered his groin. Could he mean fantasizing thinking? The idea was kind of titillating. After all, she'd been doing her own kind of thinking in the shower. And way earlier, if she was honest. Back when he'd untied her corset, she'd felt the brush of his breath across her skin and it had set every nerve ending on fire. She'd wanted to sink backward into his arms and let him slowly peel the clothing from her body. And that fantasy had nothing on what she'd imagined in the shower.

"So, um, are you going to share?"

He shook his head. "I'm a man of mystery."

"You're a man who can have the shower if he wants."

"I do." He said it, but he didn't move.

"Um…waiting for something?"

"Yeah. I thought I'd just sit here and watch you put on a swimsuit first."

"Ha!" Then she threw an extra towel at him. "Go on. You stink."

"You'd look great in that yellow bikini there."

She looked at the garment. She'd never worn a bikini in her life. As a teen she'd been much too self-conscious to wear so little. Her brothers had teased her enough when she wore her one-piece. Then there was no time for swimming between college and her job.

"Come on," Ken said. "I'm nearsighted. I won't see a thing." He flashed her a grin that had her tingling from head to toe. "Well, not unless I get up real close."

Lord, she was thinking about it. She was thinking hard about it. But if and when she undressed for Ken, she wanted it to be sexy. Trying to put on an unfamiliar bikini was more likely to be awkward. So she just lifted her chin and said primly, "I think I'll stay in this robe, thank you." Then she walked to the window and stared out at the view.

In her imagination, he came up behind her. He undid her robe and took her slowly, from behind, right against the window. She waited, taut with anxiety and lust, but all she heard was his chuckle as he headed for the bathroom and quietly shut the door.

How could she be both disappointed and relieved?

Sighing, she went back over to the swimsuits. Did she dare? Guess so, because her hands went to the yellow bikini. A month ago she would never have worn something that skimpy. But just a week of walking around in a corset had changed her. She was bolder than before and had a confidence in her body that was completely new. That, or she was just rising to the challenge in his words.

You'd look great in that yellow bikini.

He made her want to see if she really would. And if his eyes would light up in delight when he saw her in it. Or maybe darken with lust.

She knew she was playing with fire, but she couldn't resist. Before she could change her mind, she dropped the robe and put on the bikini. Then in a fit of nervousness, she all but ran outside and jumped in the pool.

He came out ten minutes later. He, too, wore a robe and, after a glance at her in the pool, grabbed a pair of swim trunks and headed back into the bathroom. A moment later he emerged, looking a lot more fit than she expected. Nothing was left of the geek she'd first met except for the general size and build. Seeing him in loose red swim trunks—and nothing else—she could tell that his pretend swordplay had paid off. He wasn't athlete-trim, but he did have muscle definition and a nicely proportioned body.

"Very nice," she said as she grabbed hold of the edge of the pool.

"You wore the yellow bikini," he said.

"I did," she answered, though he couldn't have had any more than a glimpse of it given that she was hugging the near side of the pool.

"So let me see."

"Why? You already said I'd look great in it."

"Okay, so let me appreciate." He dropped down to the side of the pool. "You know I already think you're gorgeous. Didn't I mistake you for a supermodel when we first met?"

"A supermodel?" she laughed. "I don't think so. Not at Marilyn's agency." OMG Action! had a decent reputation, but it was a long cry from representing supermodels.

"Wow, do you split hairs or what? Come on. I'm sitting out here in all my flabby glory."

"There isn't a lot of flab."

"Right back atcha, Ali."

He was right. She was too old to be this self-conscious. Besides, she was the new Ali. The sexy, confident *queen* Ali. So she took a breath and pushed back from the side of the pool. She floated backward, letting him see all of her through the distortion of the water. Then she finally put her feet under her and stood up. The pool wasn't that deep where she was. It only came to her hips, so he got a good look. Thankfully, so did she…at his face.

She saw the curve of his lips as he smiled, and the dark appreciation in his eyes. His nostrils flared, and his fingers clenched the side of the pool. He liked what he saw. And from the sudden intensity in his eyes, she guessed that he liked it a lot.

"You're good for my ego," she said softly.

"You're hell on my self-control."

She swallowed. Right there, out in the open, was the invitation. She could tell him outright that she didn't want him to stay in control. She wanted him touching her everywhere and every way. Right now. She almost got the words out, but then there was a buzz from the intercom.

"Room service," said a voice through the intercom.

Saved by the buzz. But as he got up to allow the elevator access, she let her body slide back into the cooling water. It was time, she realized. Tonight, she was going to sleep with him.

KEN WAITED AT THE ELEVATOR for the food. He let the man push the cart in, but that was it. He didn't want anyone else nearby for even a second longer than necessary. Less than a minute later, he was back outside with her.

"Want to eat out by the pool or inside in luxury?"

"I think it's luxury either way, but I vote inside. I've gotten enough sun these last few days."

"You got it." He ducked back inside, keeping an eye on her luscious body as she toweled off. Hard not to get distracted with that beautiful sight right through the screen door. Somehow he managed to get the cart unloaded, putting plates onto the table in record time.

"You must have been a waiter at some point in your life," she said as she came into the room.

He frowned. "What? No."

"Come on. You dressed that table like a pro."

He looked down at the tablecloth, settings and flowers, then chuckled. "I wasn't a waiter, but my stepmother was. Every dinner at home, she made me bus the table."

"She taught you well," she said as she sat down.

"Good to know. That way I'll have a fallback if my business goes belly-up." He meant it as a joke. It *was* a joke, but he could tell by the way she bit her lip that he'd thrown a damper on the conversation. "Hey, don't worry—"

"If you say *my* salary's secure, I swear I will hit you. I'm not worried about *my* pay."

He swallowed, unaccountably touched. "Actually, I was going to say, don't worry. There's still plenty of time to turn sales around. We started the promo a little late."

"You did?"

He nodded. "Normally we'd have started pushing at least a month earlier, but the pieces weren't in place."

She frowned, and he recognized her figuring-things-out face. Sure enough, she put the pieces together quickly enough. "You mean you hadn't found the actors yet."

He hadn't found *her* yet, but why belabor the point? "We were delayed because I was picky, yes. But I count the time well spent."

"I sure hope so," she muttered.

"I *know* so. You've been bringing in customers by the boatload."

She still had that face on. "It doesn't matter how many I bring in, though. The few hundred or so I'm converting won't make a difference on a national scale."

"Don't underestimate the value of a few hundred and good word of mouth. In the internet age, a good event gets talked about way more than you think."

She nodded. "That's good. And I guess that a groundswell

could happen at any time. In the long run, a month or two sooner or later doesn't make any difference."

He smiled. Lord, he got hard as a rock when she said stuff like that. She was *smart,* and besides that, she understood business at an intuitive level. He'd met MBAs who couldn't follow his train of thought as well as she did.

But rather than lose himself in admiring her—something he was all too prone to do—he quickly sat down and started uncovering dishes. Lord, the lasagna smelled heavenly.

"Wow, that looks good!" she said. She was looking at his plate, not her salad.

"Want to share?" he asked, pushing his plate toward her.

"Nope. I'm saving room for dessert."

"Your loss," he said as he dug in.

In the end, she did end up taking a few bites, but mostly because he insisted. Then they both tucked into the desserts.

He made the decision quickly enough. It happened sometime between her moaning at her first taste of the silk pie and when she fed him a dripping spoonful of lava cake and ice cream. In many ways, the decision had been inevitable since he'd first seen her in the hall weeks ago.

He was going to sleep with her. A lot of times in a lot of ways. That wasn't the decision. What he decided right then was that he wanted to marry her.

And that thought scared him to the opposite side of the couch.

12

ALI LOVED THE SHOW. She loved hanging out with Ken. And she really loved the way he looked at her when all she wore was a bikini and a robe.

She shouldn't have done it. He was being all noble and sitting on the opposite side of the couch from her. But it wasn't that large a couch. And while they started out sitting all prim and proper, she relaxed as she got into the show. He did, too, resting his arm on the back of the couch. That gave her room to slide sideways—not on purpose—then she tucked her legs up beneath her. For warmth.

He leaned back a little farther, stretching his legs out. And then she was startled by a scary moment. That meant she jumped—sideways, of course—straight into his arms. Within another ten minutes, she was leaning against him, her head resting back against his shoulder, and all but purring in her contentment.

Then the show ended. She sighed in regret, knowing that she would have to leave the circle of his arms. That she would have to get dressed in that corset and dusty shift and go back to her hotel room. Just because she wanted to spend the night didn't make it a good idea. They'd hit a nice balance. She didn't want to upset that. So the last thing she should do was look up at him with lust in her eyes and invite him to kiss her. The very last thing she should do.

She did it anyway. She heard him release a sigh that she couldn't interpret. Relief, surrender, desire? Any and all of those applied to herself. It didn't matter. In a moment, his mouth was on hers and she was giving herself up to him.

His arm dropped to her back and he pulled her tighter against him. She felt his tongue thrust into her mouth, and she dueled with him. Normally her mind started thinking things as she kissed. It was a normal thing for her—a brain that would not shut up. But with him, all that mental noise stuttered to a stop. Her attention was on the thrust of his tongue, the pull of his arm and the way he supported her as he gently rolled her back so he could kiss her more deeply.

She let him do it. She'd wanted this for so long and now, finally, he was pushing her onto her back. Her robe gaped, just as she'd hoped it would. He broke the kiss to press more along her cheek, the line of her jaw and down to her neck. She shivered at the feel of his hot breath, the wetness of his tongue and the erotic caress of his mouth. Every inch he touched felt electrified. And that current was transmitted to every quivering cell in her body.

Her robe was open. She still had the bikini on underneath, but that still left lots of tingling skin for his hands to stroke. And when his mouth made it to her collarbone, he pulled back, his eyes dark while his hands tightened where they touched her waist.

"I was right," he murmured. "You do look fantastic in that bikini."

"Thanks," she said, not having any other word to use because most of her mind was on the smooth expanse of his chest. She was stroking the robe off his body, too, and he shrugged it off without breaking eye contact.

"It's beautiful," he said. "May I take it off you?"

"Yes, please."

And just like that, his fingers left her waist to untie the strings that held the tiny scraps of yellow on.

The air hit her breasts and her nipples tightened painfully. Or perhaps it was the way he looked at her that made them so hard. He was reverent as his palms came to her breasts.

Oh, he had nice hands—large and dexterous. She really liked what he did with her breasts. The way he held them was nice enough, but he did something with his fingers on her nipples. She didn't have the focus to know what, but it was like he was playing with them. Tweaking them, pulling them, moving them around. It was bizarre, and it made her giggle. It also made her so wet she wanted to slide right off the couch and onto him. All the way on.

"You're not supposed to be laughing," he said, his eyes dancing.

"You're supposed to be naked," she said.

"I—" He swallowed. He was thinking. She saw all the signs of it. The way his eyes narrowed, his brow furrowed a bit and, worst of all, the way his hands stilled. She couldn't have that.

She reached out and smoothed the lines in his forehead. "Don't think, Ken. You think too much."

"One of us should."

"No. Really we shouldn't." Then she surged forward and kissed him again. As deep and thorough as she could manage. She heard him groan, and his hands slid to her waist, gripping her hips.

Yes! She pulled him closer, but she didn't have the angle. Her legs weren't spread and he was on his knees next to the couch.

On his knees? When had that happened?

She felt his thumbs hook beneath the hip straps, slowly tugging them down. Perfect. Pushing forward, she took her weight on her legs and slowly stood up. With his hands right there, the bottom half of the bikini slid right down to her knees. And as an added bonus, she stripped out of her robe at the same time.

They'd had to break the kiss as she moved, but his mouth was right there at her belly, kissing her skin while her muscles quivered beneath his touch. When he started to kiss her lower, she leaned down, tugging at his arms.

"There's a bed right over there."

He looked over, then back up at her. She swore she could see his heart in his eyes. The lust and the need. But there was something infinitely sad in them, too. She was about to ask when he answered her unasked question.

"I don't have any condoms."

Oh, hell. She'd bought some, too, just in case. But they were back in her hotel room. She hadn't thought they'd end up at a different hotel.

Wait… "It's a high-end hotel. They've got to have them somewhere in here." She frowned as she looked around. Bedside table? Bathroom? "The gift shop certainly."

"Do you want me to call room service? I'm sure they'd bring some up."

She bit her lip, thinking furiously. Then her eyes happened to fall on where her corset was lying beside the bed. Nearby was a neat stack of his clothing, both costumes complete with long leather ties. Hell, his outfit even included a modern belt.

She bit her lip, thinking. Would he go for it? They hadn't even had normal sex yet, much less her brand of fantasy play. But the idea had taken root. In truth, she'd thought of it the very first day in the leather shop. It had grown more detailed in the nights since.

"There's something I haven't told you," she said.

His eyes widened with wariness. "That sounds ominous."

She half laughed, half shrugged. "Here's the thing. I was the only child of a single mom for the first ten years of my life. I was alone a lot, read a lot, and I developed this great imagination."

He nodded, but it was clear he didn't understand. She would have to make herself more clear.

"This great fantasy life."

She knew the exact moment he understood. His body jerked slightly, but not away. It seemed as though he'd just stopped himself from leaping on her, and that made her libido all the more bold. Then he had to clear his throat before he could speak.

"Fantasy life as in…sexual fantasies?"

She nodded. "There's lots of things we can do that wouldn't involve a condom. I mean, if you want to."

He nodded slowly, but his eyes had taken on a dark kind of intensity. "I want," he said, his voice thick enough to be a growl.

"Good," she said. "Because so do I." Then she stepped back from him, using the motion to completely step out of her bikini bottoms so that she now stood naked before him. She wasn't normally this bold, but this was her summer of fantasy play. Apparently, the Ali who wore yellow bikinis and leather corsets was a lot more confident about her body than normal Ali.

She took a deep breath. "Look, this is about distracting you, right? Keeping you from going nuts worrying about your company, right?"

He straightened slowly until he stood right in front of her. He was still wearing his bathing trunks, though the robe was gone, and his erection made an impressive tent to the fabric.

"I haven't thought about my company in a few hours, Ali. I swear."

"Good. Let's keep it that way." Then she jerked her head at the bed, amazed by her own boldness. "Go lie down on the bed. And lose the shorts while you're at it."

"Um—"

"And don't you say a damn thing about work or anything

else. We're total strangers tonight. No relationship except whatever it takes to keep your mind off...other stuff."

He paused, his hand going to her cheek in a slow stroke that had her toes curling into the carpet. "Except we do have a relationship. We're—"

"Friends. With benefits." She wasn't prepared to admit to anything else just yet. Because if she did, her mind would skip straight to the real problem: What would happen to their relationship after the end of the summer? So she held it at bay, focusing instead on a stranger fantasy.

"Ali—"

"I know you think this is unethical, but honestly, I don't care. I want to live something I've dreamed about forever."

His eyebrows shot up. "You've dreamed about...about..."

"A guy, spread-eagled on his back on the bed. You can be a stranger, my boss, a vampire or a leprechaun for all I care."

"I pick stranger," he said with a laugh. "Definitely the best option."

She laughed as he started moving for the bed, his expression both intrigued and a little frightened. He paused with one leg on the bed as he turned to look at her.

"You've been dreaming about that?"

"You have no idea," she drawled.

"Apparently not."

"I have hidden depths."

He grinned. "I like hidden depths."

"Really?" she said as she grabbed his belt and her corset ties. "Are you sure? Because I'm about to tie you down."

He barely hitched as he sat down. "I should have expected that."

"You're a smart guy. I bet you kinda already did."

He assumed the position, and yes, his erection was very impressive. Meanwhile, he gave her a challenging look. "Maybe. Do I get to tie you down later?"

She paused, then shook her head. "I don't think so. Because

I don't make promises to strangers." Then she went about the business of tying him to the bed.

It wasn't as easy as it seemed. The bed was ridiculously huge and she didn't know much about knots. But he lay obediently still as she used what she had to rope him down spread-eagled. He could break out easily. A twist of his wrists or a good hard jerk of either leg would release him, but that wasn't the point. It was all about the illusion of having the man strapped down and at her mercy.

Ali stepped back to admire his body. Lying on his back like that, she could see every hill and valley cut by his muscles. He wasn't bulky. She'd known that. But there was a leanness to him that became clear in this position. Especially with the hard jut of his penis.

Wow, he was rather nice-looking. And what was even nicer was the way his penis twitched when she came close, moisture already seeping from the tip. Without even looking at the dark hunger in his eyes, she knew he was half a breath away from throwing her down on the ground and taking her, condom or not.

She grinned. "You need to picture me in a black leather corset, stiletto boots and…um…a whip in my hand."

He flinched. "Really? Can't I just go with what's really here. I like that better anyway."

She blinked, pleased by his statement. So maybe she didn't need to play up the bondage part of it. Maybe she just needed to get to what she wanted to do.

"Here's the thing, Ken doll—"

"Oh, God, don't call me that."

Without even thinking, she reached out and flicked his penis with her fingers.

"Ow!"

"I'll call you whatever I want, Ken doll."

"Okay. Okay. Don't damage the…um…attributes."

She arched her brow. "I've heard guys name it all sorts of different things. I never thought I'd hear *attributes*."

"I have a very literate soul," he said primly.

She smiled. "Okay, literate Ken. Here's what I've always wanted to do. I'm going to climb on top of you—"

"I like that—"

"In reverse."

"Oh. Uh—"

"And if you please me, I'll suck on your...attribute. If you don't please me—"

"I get it. I swear I'll work very hard to be pleasing."

"Good idea." Then she just stood there. Good Lord, was she really about to do this? Sure she'd imagined it a thousand times, but she'd also imagined herself as a kick-ass demon huntress, too. Or as a supersecret spy or even a mild-mannered librarian. She had a rather rich, erotic, literature-inspired fantasy life. But that didn't mean she was any of those things in real life.

"Hey, stranger," Ken said, effectively cutting into her thoughts. "You have to swear to never repeat a word of this to anyone else ever. It would be rather, um—"

"Embarrassing?"

He nodded. "In fact, as far as I'm concerned, this night is *not* happening. I've already forgotten it."

She nodded, realizing that he'd just said the one thing to give her the courage to act on her fantasy. Anonymous sex play it was. And she was thrilled with the idea.

She stepped forward, but he twitched on the bed, holding out his hand to stop her as best as he could.

"Swear!"

"I swear, Ken. Not a word to anyone. You?"

"Never, ever. God, I'd never hear the end of it."

She grinned, then she climbed up on the bed.

13

ALI COULDN'T BELIEVE she was doing this. Sure, the kissing and teasing was easy. She kissed Ken's lips, took her time down his torso, then even played with his enormous erection for a bit. But then she went for what she really wanted.

She straddled his face while keeping her hand and mouth by his penis. He was tied down, so he couldn't move much. Which left her in complete control.

It was amazing. When she wanted to be pleasured, she simply lowered herself to him. His tongue was very clever and completely fearless. No delicate taste for him. He stroked her, sucked her, even thrust his tongue into her, making her go wild above him.

And when it got too much for her, she just lifted up. Her thighs were quivering, her back arching, but nothing stopped her from letting him do such marvelous things to her. Nothing, that is, except when she wanted to make it last. And she wanted to make it fun for him, too.

So she would lift away from him and play with his penis just as he had played with her. Lips, teeth, tongue, she used them all. And had the satisfaction of hearing him groan whenever she engulfed him. His hips were bucking beneath her. And she was so hot that she could barely support herself. Which meant it was time.

She lowered herself back down and felt her eyes roll back in her head as he began stroking her again. Her bottom was tightening, her breath was coming in short gasps, but she didn't forget him. She started to suck on him, doing whatever she could manage for him.

She heard him groan something, but the blood was roaring in her ears. She couldn't hear him. But she felt his last rough stroke of his tongue and she went flying.

Yes!

He was mere seconds behind her, and it was so good. For both of them, she thought, but it was hard to tell beneath her general tide of *yippee!*

She collapsed to the side, flushed and hot and happy. She lay there, luxuriating in the sweetness of it all. Had she just lived out a fantasy for real? Who knew she could be that daring?

Then she cracked open her eyes and saw that he was equally dazed, his gaze unfocused, his body sated. And there was that happy little grin on his face.

"Good?" she asked when she could find the energy to speak.

"Oh, yeah," he groaned. Then with a twist of his wrists, he escaped from his bonds. So much for her knot-tying ability. But he didn't go far. Just enough to stroke his fingers along the outside of her thigh.

"Mmm," she said in response.

She thought she heard his contented sigh, but it might have been her own. Either way, she drifted into sleep for a bit. The next time she opened her eyes was when she felt him shift. Her eyes opened, and she saw he was trying to get a blanket. But it was hard to grab given she was half lying on top of him and they were both on top of the covers.

Forcing herself to move, she straightened to a better position. But then her gaze caught on the pool. And right here was another fantasy. Skinny-dipping. She'd never swum naked outside before. And now was her chance.

"Wanna catch a mermaid?" she asked.

He blinked. "What?"

"That'd be me," she said with a giggle as she scrambled off the bed and headed for the pool. She'd only covered three steps before she heard him leap off the bed. She glanced behind her.

Yes, he had *leaped* off the bed and was dashing right for her. With a squeal of laughter, she scrambled for the sliding door out to the pool. She had it open and was jumping into the water barely an inch away from his grasping hand.

The water wasn't any escape, though. He landed in the pool beside her, and then he had her.

"Caught," he said as he pulled her flush up against his body.

Ooh! Wet, slick, hard manly planes. She liked his naked body in water. Apparently he liked hers, too, because he slowly backed her up against the side of the pool then proceeded to press all his lovely body flush against her.

"You are amazing," he said as he lowered his mouth to hers. But he didn't close the deal. Not yet. Instead, he rubbed his nose against hers and slid his hands down to her hips and thighs, gently tugging them open. She'd already spread her legs to keep herself upright, but with the water below her and him bracing her against the wall, she didn't need them. Without her consciously deciding to do it, she opened herself up to him, sliding her knees up along his flanks.

He didn't waste any time pressing against her. Not into her, just his long, hard length against her folds.

"Oh, God, Ken, you're good."

She felt his mouth curve into a grin. "I've waited my whole life to hear a woman say that to me."

She stroked her thumbs along his cheeks and kissed him

hard and deep. But she froze when she felt his organ shift. She pulled back abruptly, but there was nowhere for her to go.

"Ken!" she cried.

He froze. "I'm clean, Ali. Completely healthy."

She nodded. "So am I, Ken. But…but I can't risk a baby. I won't."

He nodded, though he didn't move his lower body. Not into her, nor away. Instead, he dropped his forehead against hers.

"I want you so bad," he said. "In every way possible."

She smiled, her insides warming to molten. "I've waited my whole life to hear a man say that to me."

He lifted his head and looked her in the eyes. They were so close, she felt as though she could see straight into his soul.

"Do I call down to the front desk? They can bring us up a whole carton of condoms if we want."

She giggled, which had her bobbing precariously close to danger. "A whole carton is rather ambitious, don't you think?"

"Not with you. I feel like I could go forever with you."

She grinned. "You stud muffin, you!" Then she sobered at his intense look. He wasn't interested in teasing right now. She could feel his taut muscles and knew he was holding himself back for her sake. But he didn't want to.

Part of her didn't want him to. Part of her wanted him deep and hard inside her right now. But another part was pushing to the surface, forming words and thoughts that she struggled to express.

"I really like you, Ken," she said softly. "I really like you a lot."

"Good, because the feeling's mutual."

"But—"

He groaned and closed his eyes. "But I'm your boss."

"That doesn't make a damn bit of difference to me," she said, a little startled by her own admission. She didn't believe in office romance. Or rather, she believed that it was a bad idea on all levels. But this had never felt like a real job to her. It was more like that fun thing I did on my summer vacation. So why not bed the hottie in charge? "Really, Ken, it doesn't matter in the least bit to me that you're my boss."

His eyes lightened with hope. "So, does that mean…?"

"It means the problem is deeper than that. And believe me, I know it doesn't make sense given what we just did inside."

He got a wolfish grin on his face. "I liked what we did inside. I liked it a lot."

She felt her face heat. Yeah, that was one dream come true that more than lived up to her expectations. "The thing is, tonight was about distracting you from…everything else."

"Ali—"

"No, listen. Tonight was a moment out of time in a summer out of time."

He nodded but he clearly didn't understand what she was getting at. She didn't blame him. She was groping in the dark for what she meant, too.

"The thing is, doing the rest—the normal rest—"

"Making love."

She bit her lip, an unwelcome rush of anxiety shivering down her spine. "Yeah, doing that isn't about being out of time. It's about—"

"Being serious. With another person."

"For real. Not for fantasy play, but—"

"Real life. Real relationship."

"And then what happens at the end of the summer?"

He didn't speak, but she could tell he understood. And from the way he was easing back from her, she knew neither of them was ready to face those choices. Not yet.

"Ken, I know that doesn't make a lot of sense."

He sighed. "It makes perfect sense. I'm just having a hell of a time convincing my dick."

She laughed, as she knew he'd intended. "That's okay 'cause I gotta say—"

"Don't say it!" he cried, his expression half desperate, half terrified. "If you say you want me, too, nothing is going to keep me off you."

"Oh," she said, biting her lip. That was exactly what she'd been about to say. "How about this? I'm going to get dressed and call a cab."

Now he really did look panicked. "What? Why?"

"Because I've got the first shift tomorrow morning. Because you're the boss."

"You said you didn't care about that."

"I don't. But others will."

He sighed. He knew it was true. She could see it on his face. "Ali, I want to keep seeing you."

"We've got the rest of the summer, Ken. Seeing me is not going to be difficult."

"You know what I mean."

She did. She knew exactly what he meant, and she wanted it, too. But she didn't know how to keep the various parts of her life separate. How did she date her boss, stay professional and still explore this newfound daring of hers? And how did she guard herself so that she wasn't a complete mess at the end of the summer?

"Dinner," she said. "A simple dinner date. Just you and me. We're going to be in Chicago next, right?"

He nodded.

"I've got a cousin there I'm going to pretend to visit. You're going to do business stuff. We'll meet up at a restaurant somewhere and have a normal date."

"I can do that."

"Good. So can I."

"Okay," he said. "A normal dinner date. But I'll pick you up in a cab behind the hotel."

She smiled. "Works for me."

"Just one more thing," he said as he slid right back up to her, bracing his hands on either side of her so that she was trapped between them.

"What?"

"I want to make you come one more time."

"Ken!" she cried, but it was too late. His mouth was on her breasts and he was tonguing her nipple. She arched her back. Her body was already simmering.

Then his hand was between her legs, his fingers thrusting deep inside her. She grabbed on to his shoulders. It was her only support except for where her back was against the tile.

He started rubbing her clit with his thumb. She cried out, her entire body tightening. He was wonderfully relentless. Stroke after stroke built the fire in her blood.

She came, but he was the one who cried out.

"Yeah!"

It was another hour of pool play before she found the strength to leave. Fortunately, that was enough time for her to return the favor to him.

The last thing he said to her before she left was "this is the best damn day of my life. But dinner in Chicago—that's going to be way better."

"Bold words," she taunted from the doorway. "Sure you can live up to them?"

He grinned. "Watch me."

14

"Hey, Ali! Got a second?"

Ali had just waved goodbye to a pair of enthusiastic new customers. And while she knew she was supposed to be cheerful and available to everyone—including fellow members of the cast—what she really wanted to do was go inside the booth and sit down for...oh, a year or so. But instead, she turned around with a smile that was feeling decidedly strained. Only an hour more to go on her shift.

"Sure, Blake. What's up?"

He flashed her one of his megawatt smiles, and, as always, Ali noticed that he was a pretty, pretty man. Blond good looks, a beautifully bulked-out torso and warm honey eyes that were more golden in the sunlight than brown.

"You're off in like an hour, right?"

She nodded. "Hallelujah. My feet are about to give up the ghost."

"Yeah, I get that." Then in a display that was decidedly *not* warrior-like, he dropped the tip of his weapon into the dirt. "And this thing is *heavy*."

"Well, at least you're getting a good tan." His costume required nothing up top and relatively little down below. Some days were leather pants, but in this heat, he'd opted for the leather shorts and boots. If it wasn't for the way he wielded his sword—usually with much more respect than where it was now—he looked more like a calendar pinup guy than Sir Lancelot.

He looked down at his sculpted and now golden-tan abs. "It's a living," he quipped.

"Yeah," she echoed back in the all-too-common actor refrain. "Somebody's got to do it. Thank God it's us!"

He grinned at her, but the expression was short-lived. And, as his dazzling smile faded, he took her arm and led her a couple of steps away from the booth. She thought he was heading for the relative shade of a nearby tree, but Samantha was there chatting with Paul and Tina. Blake did a sudden side step and they were heading for a booth that sold mead.

"Want one?" Blake asked.

Ali shook her head. It wasn't that she disliked mead. The honey-based drink was rather lovely. But the day was sweltering, she was tired and adding alcohol on top would just be dangerous. She'd end up...well, living out her fantasies on top of her boss or something. Not that that hadn't been amazing, but she was with Blake now, not Ken.

"I'll take a lemonade," she said.

Blake nodded and ordered a lemonade for her and a mead for him. He paid, too, which was rather nice. And then when he turned around to hand her the drink, he flashed her his nervous smile. It was every bit as beautiful as his megawatt smile, but it had an underlying note of vulnerability in it. And it made him look all the more boyish in a gorgeous sort of way.

"So, ah," he said, "I was wondering what you're doing tonight. We both get off shift in an hour."

"Nothing much," she said, which was a lie. She intended to relive every moment of what she and Ken had done together from beginning to end. With a special emphasis on the pool play because...well, why not? "What's up?"

"Well, I thought you'd maybe like to go out."

"Sure. Tina said something about—"

"Not with everyone else," he said, cutting in. "Just me. And you."

She blinked, taking a moment to process his words. "Like on a date?"

He winced and put a hand to his heart. "Ouch! You wound me, fair Guinevere."

"No!" she cried, though she wasn't sure what she was reacting to. Had he really just asked her out for a date? "I just didn't think you'd…that I'd…" She swallowed and tried to gather her thoughts. "I just didn't think you were into my type of girl." In the short time they'd been on tour together, Ali had seen Blake go after every gorgeous woman around, and she didn't mean in the tour group. She meant the customers. And in all fairness, he'd flirted with the not-gorgeous ones, too. Old, young, pretty, plain—he'd charmed them all with his smiles, his gentle teases and his infinite amount of charisma. But it was the stunning women with the svelte bodies and the come-hither smiles that he seemed to put extra effort into. To the point that he followed them around like a puppy on a chain.

"I'm afraid to ask—what do you think my type is?" he asked.

"The really pretty ones," she answered without hesitation.

He blinked. "Have you looked in a mirror lately?"

"Now you're just stroking me."

"Wow, Ali. No self-esteem issues there."

Ali bit her lip, both embarrassed and flattered. Then, for some bizarre reason she could not fathom, her gaze slipped sideways to the booth where, inside, Ken was working.

Blake must have seen her look and misinterpreted it because he was quick to reassure her. "It's okay with them."

Ali looked back. "With whom?"

"The bosses. Ken and Paul and Tina. And actually…" He flashed a self-conscious smile. "It was Paul's idea."

"Paul thinks you and I should go out?"

He shrugged. "Publicity campaign, remember? Guinevere and Lancelot dating in real life? If we snap a picture or two, then we can leak it to the blogs."

"So you're asking me out on a date to help the campaign?" She didn't know whether to be insulted or just amused.

"You've got to learn to play the paparazzi. Use them."

She pointedly looked around at the decided *lack* of cameras. "I don't think the rag mags are interested in us."

"So we help them. Come on. Let's just do it." He flashed her his come-hither smile. "I figured I'll get us a cab about an hour after we're done here. We'll go out for a nice dinner. Talk. You know, have a normal, everyday date."

"With the paparazzi."

"No. With a camera."

What could she say? If it helped the campaign, then she had to agree. Especially given Ken's worries the night before. Looking to the side, she caught sight of Paul watching them from his place under the tree. When he realized she was looking at him, he gave her the thumbs-up and an encouraging nod.

She returned the gesture. Anything to help sales. "I guess we're on."

"Great!" Blake said as he hefted his sword. "Dress nice. We'll go someplace that serves steak!"

BLAKE SHOWED UP at her door about twenty minutes late. Not a big deal. She used the time to fuss with her makeup for the ten-zillionth time. She was so used to the stage makeup now that her everyday stuff seemed too light, too subtle, too... not her anymore. But when she put it on heavier, she just looked like a preteen after her first attempt with her mother's cosmetics.

He smiled when he saw her, gave her outfit a once-over and then asked, "Is that what you're wearing?"

She looked down at her bright yellow sundress and brown sandals. She thought she looked nice. "Um, yeah. Why?"

"Oh, nothing. It looks great on you. You look great. I was just thinking that we clash." He gestured vaguely to his black denim jeans and silver silk shirt.

Ali frowned. She didn't think they clashed exactly, but he was right. They certainly didn't match. She was dressed summer dinner and a movie. He was dressed Hollywood night-club chic.

"Did you want me to change? It'll only take me a second."

He bit his lip, obviously thinking. Then he shook his head. "No, I'm being ridiculous. This is supposed to be a real date. And besides, the cab is waiting."

Of course it was. Because he'd been twenty minutes late. But she grabbed her purse, regretting that she didn't have a slim golden date purse. She did at home, but she hadn't brought it with her because, really, she hadn't expected to change months of datelessness while on tour. Guess she'd been wrong!

She watched his face, noting that it remained carefully neutral when she grabbed her brown leather purse with the painted butterflies on it. She'd found it at an art fair years ago and loved it. But it was, sadly, a little worse for wear.

"I'm sorry," she said. "I don't have a different purse."

"What? Oh, that's okay. I barely noticed." A lie if there ever was one. But he was smiling at her and his words were sweet even if she did know he was lying. Then he offered her his arm and they walked down the hallway like Ginger Rogers and Fred Astaire.

They got in the cab and he had to fumble with his iPhone as he tried to pull up the nearest steak house. In the end, she asked the cabbie to recommend someplace. He took them to a lovely restaurant with a fireplace and open grills. It felt rather Texan in its decor, and Ali suppressed a tiny squirm of disappointment. After all, she'd lived her entire life in Texas. It would have been nice to go to a restaurant that served something different.

They were escorted to their table and Blake looked around. "Rustic. Fun, but rustic."

"We can poke fun at the decor," she offered. "Decide if it's *real* Texan or just fake."

"Good idea. The antlers on the chandelier—fake."

"Thank God. I'd hate to think of—" she quickly counted the number of antlers shoved together to decorate the lighting fixtures "—thirty or more bucks being shot just to hide a lightbulb or two."

"The Stetson's real. Just real lame."

She wasn't sure about lame. It was just odd hanging there on the wall for decor. The people she knew who wore cowboy hats actually wore them. But they didn't hang them high on the wall as if they were supposed to be art.

The waiter came, and they placed their drink orders. Then Blake started a running talk on his last gigs. Ali listened, made polite comments, but soon her mind was wandering. She liked Blake and all, and he was certainly hot to look at, but it just wasn't the same as going out with Ken. Mostly because Blake talked about himself. A lot.

"Oh, God," Blake exclaimed, "I've bored you to tears. I'm not surprised. I've been gabbing away, and not finding out more about you. Which was the whole point, by the way. Finding out about you."

Ali blinked. "What? Why?" Okay, so that wasn't the most come-hither response she'd ever made. "I thought this was a publicity event."

"Well, it's that, too," he said. "Speaking of which…" He pulled out his cell phone and aimed it to take a picture. "Lean in close."

She did, and he snapped a picture only to look at it, frown, then make her do it all over again. About a dozen times.

"Blake…" she began as he stared at the last picture.

"It just looks too posed. And the resolution isn't good."

"Because it *is* posed and you're using a cell phone."

He nodded. "It's supposed to look like we were caught sneaking out. Let's get the waiter to take the shot."

And so it was done. Fortunately the restaurant wasn't that busy. The waiter was extremely patient as Blake made him take a zillion different shots. He paged through them as their food came.

"This one will work," he said as he showed it to her. But before she could get a good look, he had flipped to the next. "This one's awful. But you look good."

"I think you always look good."

He laughed. "Nice thought, but good isn't going to get me to Hollywood."

"That's where you want to be?"

"Isn't it obvious? I'm hoping this summer tour will get me some exposure. Better than summer theater, in any event."

"Blake—"

"Actually, it's Brian, but don't tell anyone."

"What?"

He laughed. "My real name is Brian. Boring old Brian. Not even with a *y*. So when I decided to go into acting, I took up a stage name to spruce it up."

"But Brian is a lovely name."

"Maybe. But it's the guy I'm trying to get away from, not who I want to be."

She set down her fork to concentrate better. "I don't understand."

He grinned. "Of course not. Because you're genuine. You like who you are, you're comfortable with it, and you don't look to everyone else for validation."

She blinked. That was unexpectedly deep, and she wasn't at all sure it fitted her. "Of course I want to change who I am. I want to be prettier, bolder, stronger in every way." That was, after all, a big part of why she'd decided to go on this Summer of Strutting in a Corset. It was so she could be more of everything she wanted to be.

He nodded. "But you're just doing the superlatives. I'm doing the *out*."

"Huh?"

He popped a bite of steak into his mouth, then gestured to her with his fork. "You're adding on to who you are. The base is set. You want to be *bolder, stronger*. I want to change completely. Erase Brian and replace him with Blake."

She frowned. "You mean the Blake that has to make sure my clothes match his, the one who is obsessed with pictures of himself and was twenty minutes late to pick me up for our date?"

He winced. "Yeah, sorry about that. I had to redo my hair like three times."

She blinked. His blond locks were gorgeous. "What was wrong with your hair?"

"The mousse was too thick, then too thin, then just all wrong. I was trying some new stuff, but…" He grimaced. "But you don't want to know about that."

"I want to know why you think Blake would be the least bit more interesting than Brian."

He sighed. "See, that's just it. Brian is obsessed with what to do to further his career. Summerfest or promo tour? Blog pictures with a girl or hot single guy at the bar? Brian is all work and no fun."

"And Blake?"

"Well, Blake is casual cool. He's quiet, noble and a real hero. He has to work out and eat well to keep his body working right, but it's not his primary focus. And Blake's career just happens because he's awesome like that."

"That sounds like a fictional character, not a real person."

Blake/Brian shrugged. "It's who I need to be to get ahead."

She processed what he'd said and tried not to compare him to Ken. Sadly, she did, and poor Blake couldn't compete with Ken's quiet confidence. "So, let me take a stab at the particulars. You were gorgeous in high school, and I know you played sports."

He nodded. "But I wasn't very good at them. I mean, I'm coordinated and all, but bashing people around in football just seemed like two walls of testosterone going at it. I really wanted to be a drama geek."

Ali toyed with her mashed potatoes, her thoughts on high school. "I didn't have the chance to play sports. The very idea was laughable in my mind. I'm just too clutzy. So I was the lighting tech."

"And the technical director, I'll bet. The one who makes sure everyone is where they need to be, and that everything is working just the way it ought."

She nodded. "I tried."

"Yeah, actors are lost without someone like you. Directors, too. You're the quiet organizers, and you're never valued enough." He snorted. "Or paid enough."

He had that so right. And he had a point. Even if no one else valued her skills, she needed to be sure she didn't undervalue herself. She lifted her chin, her self-confidence rising a notch. "Thank you," she said. "That was really nice to hear. And something I'm going to have to remember when I go back to my regular job."

He shuddered. "Don't say those horrible words."

She laughed, then turned the conversation back to him. "So what shows did you do?" she asked.

He started listing them. Soon they were lost in the realm of high-school performance stories. They even wandered into some of his football nightmares. Before long, they were both laughing and the meal flew by. As did the desserts. And the after-dinner drinks. Even the cab ride back to the hotel was filled with fun.

It wasn't until they were stopping right outside her bedroom door that things grew serious again. It was because he was going to kiss her. She could see the intention in his eyes, and she couldn't help but marvel at it. She'd been completely dateless for months, and suddenly she had a very full plate of men with Ken and Brian/Blake.

Blake was starting to lean in when she held up her hand. "This is not going to happen. I'm so sorry, but—"

"It has to, Ali. It's not newsworthy unless there's some sizzle."

She leaned back against her door and shook her head. "It's not newsworthy at all. You can't possibly believe that someone will print this."

"Someone will. Bloggers need content all the time. Ali, just once. For the camera."

She folded her arms, but he was already pulling out his camera phone. "I'm not kissing you for a blog."

"Then do it to help my career. Or Ken's product. Or because every bit of publicity helps." He waggled his eyebrows at her. "Come on. They're going to print a picture of two gorgeous people kissing because everybody likes looking at that. Especially if there's a little bit of scandal attached to it. Come on. It's Guinevere and Lancelot making time away from King Arthur."

None of that had the least bit of effect on Ali. None of it except the part about helping sell Ken's product. She couldn't forget how anxious Ken had been yesterday. And that the sales were on par with Leaper, his flopped product. She'd already sworn she'd do everything she could to help. What was the harm in a little kiss between Guinevere and Lancelot? She'd just chalk it up to acting.

"Oh, all right."

"Excellent!" he said. Then he carefully propped up his phone on a nearby fire extinguisher. A moment later, she heard the telltale beep as the timer started ticking down. Then he stepped up to her, pressed his pelvis way too hard against her, and adjusted his face for the right angle. Then he touched her cheek with his hand.

"Blake—"

"Shhh. And for you, it's Brian."

Then he kissed her. He came in too fast and she tried to pull back. But she couldn't and as she tried to push him off, he invaded her mouth. Yuck! Fortunately, she heard the click of the phone camera. Not so fortunately, Blake/Brian wasn't stopping. Or at least he didn't until she shoved him hard.

Sadly, he was really muscular so he barely moved. "Oh, Ali, you are a queen," he murmured.

Then an awful thing happened. Ken came around the corner and stopped dead, his eyes taking in the tableau of Blake with his hand on her face and both their lips wet. He went chalk-pale.

Ali shoved Blake off her. He went easily this time, damn him. Then she took a step toward Ken. "This isn't what it looks like," she said. *Oh, no! Lame, lame, lame!* she screamed at herself.

Meanwhile Blake—he'd shifted very much into his Blake persona—grabbed his phone and aimed it at Ken. "Don't be ridiculous, Ali," he said. "It looks like you and I were making out in the hallway. And got caught." Then as Ken's face shifted into a tight mask of anger, Blake snapped a picture. "And King Arthur is definitely pissed. Perfect!"

Ali all but rolled her eyes. "It's a publicity stunt," she said to Ken. "Ask Paul. It was his idea."

"Not all of it," said Blake with a suggestive leer. "Some parts we thought up all on our own!"

"Stop it!" Ali cried.

Blake laughed as he gave her a jaunty wave. "This is so going to kill on the blogs!" Then he went down the hall to his own room. Which left her standing there in the hallway with Ken.

"I swear. It was for publicity."

"I don't want that kind of publicity."

She might have said more. She would have said a lot more if she could think of what she could say, if she knew how to redeem the situation and if Ken weren't looking as though he'd just been betrayed. Which he had. But she never got the chance. He just shook his head and walked to his room.

"Ken—"

"Good night, Ali." Then he disappeared into his room.

15

KEN WAS CURSING at his computer in the back corner of another comic-book shop, this one in Chicago. The show out on the main mall stage had finished an hour ago. Fortunately, they were in the rising-suspicion stage between Arthur and Lancelot. That meant daily stage fights between the two men as Lancelot's betrayal burned between them both. Obviously, they'd taken a departure from the original legend. According to history, Lancelot and Arthur never fought against each other until they got onto opposite sides of a battlefield. But this made for a better show, especially with Paul playing Mordred and egging on the animosity.

And frankly, Ken really enjoyed trying to beat the hell out of Blake. All he had to do was bring up the memory of Blake pressing Ali up against her hotel door and Ken's aggression level soared. Made for a good show, though both men now had numerous bruises. It also made for good sales, which also helped.

But that was an hour ago. Now he was back at the comic-book shop and dealing with his own personal crisis. He was on the verge of throwing his laptop against the wall when Paul stepped in.

"Sales will pick up," he said. "We're building momentum. You'll see."

Ken blinked, then shrugged, shoving down the panic he felt deep in his belly. "Thanks," he said. "But that's not what I was cursing about."

"The website's fixed, by the way."

Ken leaned back in his chair. "Yeah, I noticed. Thanks."

Paul released a heavy sigh. "Not a problem, since I was the one who broke it in the first place."

Paul had been uploading video from their last event and had managed somehow to crash their online purchasing. The solution had required an emergency call to their web designers and about a thousand dollars, but it was up and running now. And that was only one of about a hundred other such mistakes that Paul had been making in the past month alone.

"Yeah," Ken said slowly. "So what's going on?"

"It was just a stupid mistake. Could happen to anyone."

"Maybe. But there have been a lot of stupid mistakes lately."

Paul nodded but didn't speak. As his friend, Ken didn't want to push. But as his employer with a product to launch and a company to keep afloat, Ken needed some assurances that this type of slipup wasn't going to continue. "Paul—"

"I know I've been a disaster lately. God, I know!" He rubbed his chin and looked absolutely miserable. "But I'm going to figure it out."

Ken exhaled, his mind weighing his choices here. "I can't let this kind of thing continue, Paul. I just can't."

"I know. Just please…give me a little more time. I'm figuring it out."

"Just what exactly are you figuring out?"

Paul shook his head, refusing to answer that question. "One more chance, Ken. If I screw up again, you can fire me. Or better yet, I'll quit."

"I don't want to do that," he said. And he didn't. He and Paul had been together since college.

"I know. And you won't have to. I swear."

He waited. Ken waited. They both looked at each other with the silent communication of longtime friends. And in the end, Ken nodded. Then he turned to the computer and grimaced. He considered trying to figure this out on his own, but he was desperate here, looking for a perfect date evening with Ali. Problem was, he'd been so busy with the events that he hadn't had time to properly prepare for what he wanted to do. Of course, he also had no idea what the perfect date was, so that made it extra hard.

"That doesn't look like sales projections," Paul said from right over his shoulder. "So what's got you scowling if it's not the website or the business?"

Ken glared at the computer screen. He'd been searching restaurants in Chicago, which was like finding a particular ant in an anthill. There were a zillion and he had no idea which one would provide the perfect date. He needed help. And besides, he reassured himself, there was a way to get the information he needed without giving anything away to Paul.

"So," he said, "you're familiar with Chicago, right?"

Paul's eyebrows rose. "I grew up here, but it's a big city. What are you looking for?"

"The perfect date. With a girl I met online."

Paul waited a beat. Then another beat more. Ken could see first relief on his friend's face, then laughter. Ken put on a fierce scowl to forestall the guffaws, but that only tipped his friend over into deep belly laughs.

"Fine. Don't help," Ken groused.

"No, no. I'm sorry. I'm just glad that you're worried about something other than the product. I just never thought it would be a girl you met online."

Ken was about to ask Paul to explain that statement, but then decided he really didn't want to know. "Look, it's not a big deal. I just need to know where to take her."

Paul's humor dialed back to low chuckles. "I assume you're

not talking about the kind of perfect date that can be found on bathroom walls or in the right section of the yellow pages."

"God, no! Look, I promised this girl a perfect evening. Yeah, that was stupid, but now I've got to try and live up to it."

"She's a girl in Chicago? Who?"

So here was the tricky part. Fortunately, Ken had a lie ready. "I met her online a while ago. We've been…emailing. I thought we could get together tonight."

"What kind of online?"

Ken frowned. "What do you mean what kind? On-the-internet online."

"On a dating website?"

"No!"

"Don't get huffy. There are a lot of nice girls on those sites."

Ken looked at his friend, who was working hard to appear innocent. There was a story there, but he didn't have time to pursue it.

"No. It was an…um…a chat forum."

"Really?" There was a wealth of unspoken comment in that one word and all of it was pornographic.

"No, not that kind of forum. It was a comic-book forum. You know. For collectors."

"I thought you'd stopped collecting when you were sixteen."

Mostly true and hell, lying was a lot harder than it should be. "Forget that. Tell me where I should take her for the perfect date."

"Comic-book-collector girl. From the internet. Take her someplace fun and unexpected. Collectors love the unexpected. Not too fancy. You don't want to intimidate her by going too ritzy." Paul snapped his fingers. "Go to Ed Debevic's in the city."

"Ed who?"

"It's like a Chicago landmark. If the date goes wrong,

you can say you've always wanted to try it. That you'll take her somewhere else next time." Paul waggled his eyebrows. "That'll get you set up for date two if you want it."

He'd want it, but he couldn't say that out loud. Not without risking a little too much curiosity from Paul. "You're sure?"

"Positive. It's fun. It's flirty. It's something a comic-book collector would get off on. Go late, when the crowd is more adult. It's way more fun."

No problem there. They weren't going to finish at the mall until almost nine. "What's the address?"

"Here," Paul said, pulling out his phone. "I'll text it to you."

And so it was done. Ken exhaled a sigh of relief, which lasted about two seconds because right after that, Tina came rushing back with an emergency. It wasn't a big emergency—a kid had been snooping around where he wasn't supposed to be and had tripped over some of the wiring. No biggie, but in today's world, it behooved them to make nice with the snooper's parents while involving mall security. Make sure everyone was okay, then cover their legal butt.

Not a big deal, but one that involved all of Ken's attention. Which was why—three hours later—when he was dressed in his best suit, he escorted a dazzling-looking Ali into Ed Debevic's—which was the equivalent of a raunchy burger-and-soda shop.

Oops.

WELL, THIS WASN'T AT ALL what she'd been expecting. Ali looked around the restaurant, seeing the tile floor, the chrome-and-laminate tables, the soda-shop decor. The waitresses were dressed in fifties diner dresses with aprons, and the waiters had on suspenders covered in buttons. She saw a woman in big sunglasses shaped like hearts, a plethora of white paper hats and most surprising of all, two busboys standing on the counter just finishing the song "YMCA," complete with hand motions and hip thrusts.

All in all, it looked like a fun place to get a burger and fries. But it was not at all what she'd expected. Especially since she was wearing her best dress, heels and jewelry, not to mention her makeup, which she'd taken an eternity to apply. Ken looked similarly dressed up in a great gray suit. He also looked equally surprised by the decor.

"I'm going to kill Paul," she heard him mutter.

"You told Paul we were going out?" she asked, a little startled.

"No. I said I had a date with a girl I met in an online chat forum. He recommended this place. For a first date."

"Well, it does look fun," she hedged.

"Ali, I'm so sorry. We can go somewhere el—"

"Did you two get lost looking for the opera?" asked a grinning hostess.

"Um—" Ken began, but the woman had turned to the restaurant at large and started bellowing.

"Hey, everybody! These guys were looking for the Opera House and came here. What should we do?"

The busboy who'd been doing "YMCA" jumped off the counter. "Guess they want an aria."

"We really don't—" said Ken, but it was too late.

The boy began belting out something that had to be in mangled Italian. He was really very good. His voice was pure, and his expressions were perfect comic exaggerations. In truth, he was hysterical in a Jim Carrey kind of way. By the time he finished, Ali was clapping along with everyone else.

"So, lost boy and girl," said the hostess. "Do you want a table in Neverland?"

Ken looked at her, and Ali shrugged. "You can really never have enough onion rings."

"Oh, onion breath," piped in the hostess. "Only a good idea if you both eat." Then she elbowed Ken. "What do you say, big boy? You up for a heaping pile of Screaming O?"

Ali laughed at the double entendre. It wasn't a perfect joke, but the way the woman said *O* definitely suggested *orgasm*.

"Um, yeah. I'm good with Screaming Os." He looked at Ali. "You sure?"

"Can't turn down a good O, can I?"

The hostess grinned. "I never do!"

So it was decided. They were escorted to a booth and settled down on red vinyl seats with menus that were approximately the size of the Dead Sea Scrolls.

"That's a lot of page to say cheeseburger and fries," Ken commented.

Ali grinned. "Well, they have to add in the Screaming Os, too."

"Oh, yes. Shall we share one or go for two?"

"I prefer to share my Os."

Ken was still grinning when the waiter came to take their order. They had to get it in before the hostess started singing "Over the Rainbow." By the time she was done, Ali's eyes were misting with delight. The waitress had been really good!

"I don't know about perfect date," she said, "but we've hit memorable for sure!"

"I was not going for infamy."

"I hope you were going for fun because you've hit that mark."

Ken sobered. "I'll make it up to you, I swear. We'll go someplace classy next time."

Ali shook her head. "Don't apologize. This is fun. Anybody can go classy. It takes a special date to take me over the rainbow."

Ken smiled and seemed to relax. Ali did, too, and for a moment she flashed on her date with Blake. This one was much better.

They started talking generally about the launch. She asked about sales. He hedged while the muscles around his eyes tightened. She took that to mean that sales continued to be sluggish, and he didn't want to think about it. She bit her lip, honestly intending to let it go. But the idea of financial disaster meant different things to different people, and she really wanted to know what it meant to him.

"So, um, let's say the worst happens," she said, watching his face closely for signs that she was treading on unacceptable territory. "How bad is bad? Are you going to end up homeless and eating out of trash cans?"

Ken blinked, then laughed. "Me? No. But I worry about Paul. He's not as careful with his dimes as I am. Besides, Paul has a life. He goes out on dates, wines and dines potential clients—I think on his own dollar, though I tell him to charge the business—and he generally lives the life of a charismatic man in Houston."

"And you?"

Ken shrugged. "I'm the original nerd. My mother died when I was young, so I had years with just me and my dad. He was a mechanic, but should have been an engineer. We liked nothing better than to tear stuff apart in the garage and put it back together. We tore apart lawn mowers and wet/dry vacs to build robots. If it had a motor, we tore it apart and put it back together."

"Sounds like wholesome guy fun."

"It was." His face grew wistful. "I miss those days."

"Is your father gone?"

Ken shook his head. "Worse. He remarried a woman he's crazy about."

Ali laughed. "That's bad?"

"That's great for him. But the two of them do everything together. Antiquing—her passion. Camping—his new hobby. And they're in a his-and-hers bowling league."

"The horrors!"

Ken shrugged. "It's embarrassingly cute to watch."

She nodded, listening to the note of loneliness in his voice.

"But it left you out in the cold? How old were you when they got together?"

"Fifteen. And she had kids, too, one of them troubled. He's okay now, but for a while there he was constantly in trouble."

"So good-boy Ken was left out."

"It wasn't bad. I was a teenager. Old enough to have a life of my own. I just…"

"You just missed being one-on-one with your dad. I get it. The same thing happened when my mom remarried. I like all my brothers, and I'm really close with my cousin. But the times that were just with my mom were really good."

He nodded, but she could tell his mind wasn't on his childhood. A moment later, his words confirmed it. "At this point, I don't think I'm in danger of bankruptcy. Sales are picking up. Slowly, but they're there. It's a good product. People will buy it once word of mouth gets going."

"That's a relief."

He flashed a smile that lasted less than a second. "But there's always a nagging fear of a problem, especially in this economy. Fortunately, I've got things covered for everyone."

"Everyone?" she asked, startled that he had contingency plans for his employees.

"Yeah, if QG goes belly-up, the programmers are covered. With a good recommendation from me, they'll get a job. Same with Tina. She's a genius at organization. Paul has some savings. Not as much as would make me comfortable, but that's him."

"And you?"

"Oh, I'll probably help out my dad at the garage while I figure out what to do next. I've got choices. There are a few companies that would be interested in a man of my background." He took a deep breath. "In short, if disaster happens, it will be okay. It will suck, but it'll be okay."

She reached out and touched his hand. "So why the long

face? Why the constant knot of anxiety between your eyebrows?"

He frowned then wiggled his eyebrows. "I have a knot?"

She smiled. "You do."

"Well," he said, "I guess it's because I don't want it to suck. I want to be really, really successful."

That was logical, but she sensed there was more to it than that. "Come on, Ken." She made pretend hypnotism gestures. "Tell me all."

He laughed, probably because she was trying to be funny, not because she really was. But it didn't matter. It broke the tension and got him talking again.

"I'm a nerd boy. Not quite the computer-programmer geek, but close enough. I was only average at sports, good in school, but nothing special. What I can do—what I want to do—is run a successful business. For my employees who depend on me being not-stupid with the company. For my dad who runs his own business very successfully."

"The garage?"

He nodded. "And then there's the most stupid reason of all."

She leaned forward. "Oh, I'm dying to know. What is it?"

"What every nerd-boy wants: to be rich and successful and get all the hot chicks."

She snorted. "Have you looked at your tour bus lately? You're buried in hotties."

He nodded. "Yeah…"

"But being up to your eyeballs in gorgeous models—both male and female—is not the same thing as taking them to bed."

"Or impressing them. It's very important to us nerds to impress the girls."

She smiled. "You're impressive, Ken. Trust me on this one. You're very impressive." Then she sobered, thinking through his words. "You want a wife, don't you? A house and kids. A dog and the mom-mobile van. The whole American-dream package."

"Yeah, I do. What about you? What do you dream about at night?"

She didn't have to think long about her answer. Despite the variety in her sexual fantasies, the truth was they all boiled down to one thing. "I dream about a man who loves me. That's it in a nutshell. A good man."

"To marry and have kids with? Or to rock your world in bed?"

She grinned. "Can't I have both?"

"In my world? Absolutely." Then he tilted his head and frowned at her. "Question is, why haven't you done it already?"

She blinked, startled by his question. "What do you mean?"

They had to wait a moment as their food was served. It was great. Good cheeseburger, better onion rings. They both took a few moments to stuff their faces. But all too soon, Ken was back on topic and Ali was surprised by how difficult his questions were for her.

"You're smart, organized and beautiful. College boys aren't that dumb. You would have been hit on. A lot."

"Frat boys hit on anything with boobs."

"It wouldn't have been just frat boys. There had to be others."

She shrugged and tried to take refuge in her food. But his words had unsettled something inside her. Eventually, she started to answer, though the words were difficult to get out.

"I took the risk once. It was a bad one. He was a jerk, and it nearly destroyed me when he left."

"You didn't kick him to the curb?"

She shook her head. "No, I didn't. I didn't have the strength. And I kept thinking it would somehow magically work out." She sighed. "You don't understand what I was like as a kid. I was home alone all the time until I was ten. Sure there were babysitters and stuff, but mostly I just lived in books. Then suddenly my mother remarries and I've got siblings. Younger brothers who were into everything. When I wasn't babysitting, I retreated into my room and read some more."

"Sounds lonely."

She toyed with an onion ring. "I was surrounded by family. Too much family compared to what I was used to. It wasn't until college that I forced myself out of my room."

"College does that to a person. Gets them out of their comfort zone."

"That's when I ended up feeling lonely. Then I met The Jerk who hadn't started out as an ass. A semester later I had to leave college because the money ran out, and well..."

"A bad situation became worse?"

She nodded. "It took me a while to get over The Jerk, then I was working full-time and I just don't meet that many guys."

He dropped his chin on his palm and looked at her. His expression was serious, but it was his eyes that really caught her. He was looking—at her—with all of his considerable attention and focus. It made her feel important. It also made her squirm.

"What are you thinking?" she asked.

"That there's something you're not telling me."

"There really isn't."

"It's okay. You don't have to tell me."

She shook her head. "No, I'm serious. I'm not hiding anything. There really just isn't that much to me. I read, I work, I...don't meet guys who ask me out on dates."

"I asked you out."

"A minor miracle, in my world."

"Blake asked you out."

Her food caught in her throat. "It was for a publicity stunt. He said Paul wanted us to do it."

Ken nodded, his expression excruciatingly neutral. "I know. But how did the date go?"

"It was fine except for posing for a zillion candid photos." Then she touched his hand and told him the truth. "The evening was fine, but it wasn't an evening with you."

His eyes widened, and he looked at her with those big puppy-dog eyes. Then he blinked, and the image was gone. No more puppy dog. Instead, it was a man there and his eyes were dark with hunger. The shift was so abrupt, she was momentarily taken aback by it. At least her mind was. Her body was way ahead of her, already growing liquid as she looked at him.

He slowly set down his fork. "I know I'm your boss—"

"Don't care."

"And I had wanted to keep this relationship quiet."

She nodded. That was just prudent.

"But if you want, I'd like to step things up a bit."

She swallowed, her heart speeding up until she felt it pounding in her throat. "Step it up?"

His smile came slowly, but when it hit its peak, he was more handsome than she'd ever seen. Gone was his usual geek-boy persona. The person before her now was all man. "Step it up, Ali. With me."

She looked into his eyes and saw his absolute certainty in what he was asking. He wanted a relationship with her. The kind that could end in marriage and that mom-mobile in the suburbs. She saw it right there in his eyes, and she couldn't believe how excited she was by the thought. "Yes," she suddenly forced out through her very dry throat.

"Yes?"

She swallowed and nodded.

He looked down at her plate, which had her half-eaten burger on it. "You still hungry?"

She shook her head.

"Dessert? Coffee? Want anything else here?"

Again she shook her head.

He grinned and waved to the waiter. "Check, please!"

16

KEN DIDN'T WANT TO BLOW THIS. He didn't want to screw up and say something stupid. On the other hand, he didn't want to be silent when he ought to be saying something. Which was a real problem for him because his brain was always telling him either to say something or not to say something, and the whole thing was rather unreliable when dealing with women.

So he went with his gut instead, even though it was tied in knots at the idea of confessing this particular sin.

They were outside the restaurant waiting for a cab. They were holding hands, which was the only reason he wasn't completely out of his mind with lust. She was keeping him steady and his brain relatively quiet. Mostly, he was enjoying the feel of her hand in his while his boner was gleefully anticipating another night like the last one they'd spent together.

But first he had to confess. So he took a deep breath and turned to her.

"I, um, well…did you ever wonder why you've always had a room to yourself this trip? When the other girls have to share?"

She blinked, then slowly shook her head. "I thought it was because I was the lead woman or something like that. Or because the other girls were friends."

Ken shook his head. "The others didn't know one another

before the tour and, yeah, I used the excuse of you being the lead female."

Always quick to pick up on the nuances, Ali lifted her chin. "The excuse?"

He nodded. "Despite my big stand on being your boss, I was hoping something like this would happen. And since Paul and I are sharing…" He let his voice trail off as she understood that he'd been planning to bed her from the very beginning. "I just didn't want it to be with Blake."

"I'm so sorry about all of that. I only did it—"

"For the publicity, I know. I don't know what Paul was thinking."

She released a breath. "So you did talk to Paul."

Ken nodded, then he took a deep breath. Might as well confess it all. "The truth is I heard Tina and Samantha talking about it. They said it was a date. Then, I guess I kinda stalked you. I waited for you guys to return and watched from around the corner." He grimaced. "I know. Real mature."

"I know this sounds stupid, but I only did it for you. Because Blake swore it would help get publicity for the game."

He felt a slight weight roll off his shoulders.

"And for the record," she continued, "I hated kissing him. Hated it."

A huge weight dropped to the ground with a thump. Of course, his conscious mind had known that. After all, she'd just said she wanted to up their relationship. Ergo, she had picked him over Blake. But it was really good to hear her say it. Really, really good.

He released his breath in a long, happy sigh. "And now, also for the record, we don't have to do anything—"

She stretched up on her toes and kissed him. It was a full kiss, one where she teased his lips with her tongue. And then she opened up completely as he wrapped his arms around her and dived right in. God, he loved kissing her. She seemed to love everything he did. Little nips, hard thrusts, it didn't matter. She was always flushed and breathless when he stopped.

"So…" he said when they finally separated. "You're okay with going back to your hotel room?"

She smiled and he caught a flash of real mischief in her eyes. "I'm so okay with it, I'm annoyed with the cab for taking so long."

Good. They were on the same page. "I, uh, I brought condoms this time."

She bit her lip and looked adorably flushed. It didn't take long for him to guess why.

"You have some, too, don't you?"

She shrugged. "I've had them for a while now."

He turned her to face him more fully. "Tell me now—while I still have some blood in my brain—tell me what you like."

She frowned. "Like?"

"In bed. I want to know. I mean—"

"You want to rock my world?"

He nodded. "Exactly."

Her tongue went between her teeth and again, there was that shy sparkle of mischief. "We got to live out my fantasy last time. Don't you think it's your turn?"

"You are my fantasy," he answered honestly. And he was a little startled by the truth in those words.

"But you have to have something more than that. A wish, a fantasy, something. You were a teenage boy, weren't you?"

He did. It was just that he wasn't sure she'd go with his idea of fun.

"Come on," she said with a laugh. "Spill it."

"In front of a mirror. Me behind. I want to see every part of you as…well, you know."

She grinned. "Yeah. And…um, okay."

"Okay?"

"Okay."

Okay!

THEY MADE IT TO Ali's room in record time, but it wasn't fast enough to keep Ken from doubting himself. He wanted this to be perfect for her. He wanted to *be* perfect for her. Consciously, he knew it was an impossible dream, but that didn't stop him from feeling inadequate to the task.

They were just inside her hotel-room door when he turned her to stand face-to-face with him. But he couldn't look at her directly yet, so he closed his eyes and dropped his head onto her forehead.

"I know performance anxiety is not macho," he said.

She laughed. "I've never been considered macha anyway, so why start now?"

He blinked, taking a moment to realize she was confessing to her own insecurities. "No," he said. "I was telling you I'm nervous. The last time was so incredible…" He shook his head, still awed by that particular memory.

"That was fun, wasn't it?" she whispered and even if he couldn't see her mischievous smile, he heard it in her voice.

"I want this to be equally good for you."

She blew out a low whistle. "That's a pretty tall order."

He groaned. "I know."

Then she pushed up on her toes enough to give him a quick kiss. "So how about we make this about fulfilling your fantasy?"

"But—"

"Come on…" she said, taking hold of his hand and drawing him deeper into her bedroom. "Tell me it from the beginning."

He felt his face heat to burning. "Really? You want to hear it…in detail?"

She glanced over her shoulder at him. Lord, she was beautiful when her eyes sparkled like that. "How else can I act it out?"

He turned her around again, pulling her into his arms. She warmed him. She got him to stop thinking. She made everything seem fun and good.

So he kissed her. He touched her cheek, lifted her face just enough and then pressed his mouth to hers. She opened easily to him, and he felt as if she were giving him this great gift. His fantasy. But also something more. Her heart.

It was a silly, girlie thought. He did *not* think about hearts and love and things like that. Sure he wanted it, but mostly he lived in a world of accounting tables and product-performance charts.

But with her, he thought of things like that. And he wanted things like that. And he wanted…to slowly take off her clothing. Slowly. Sensuously. While he watched every inch of her—front and back—with the help of the mirror.

"Are you sure you're up for this?" he whispered. His hands were already busy, stroking her shoulders, sliding down her arms and then reaching up behind her back. He had the zipper of her dress in his fingers, but he didn't pull.

Meanwhile, she bit her lip as she slid her hand down his belly until she outlined his erection. "I think we're both up for it."

That was all the confirmation he needed. So while he could still think—and coordinate the use of his hands—he pulled down the zipper of her dress.

She wore a very silky-feeling dress with a V-neck in front and a flirty skirt. There was some sort of pattern on it, but he really didn't care what. What he noticed was the way it showed off her legs and emphasized her cleavage. And now, wonder of wonders, he was watching it slip off her shoulders and down.

The hotel half mirror was behind her and he stood facing her, so he got to see both sides as a white lacy bra appeared and matching shortslike panties cupped her very sexy ass.

He stepped backward to admire and ran smack into the edge of the bed. She laughed as he stumbled slightly, and then she shoved him quick and hard on the shoulders. Down he went onto the bed, sitting there while she stood tall and proud before him.

"Take off your jacket," she ordered.

He grinned as he complied. He liked this take-charge attitude of hers. Then, before he could fully shed his jacket, she got hold of his tie and dragged him forward for another full kiss. She ended it much too soon for him, and stepped back to look at him.

"You going to dance for me?" he asked.

She blinked, apparently startled. Then he watched the blush creep up her chest into her face. "Uh…" she began.

"Don't worry about it. Dancing's overrated. I really like—"

"To watch?"

"To touch. Hard to do if you're moving all around." Then he fitted words to action. He pulled her toward him by her hips, extending his fingers around her waist and curving them down toward her very lovely bottom. "You have the smoothest skin."

She smiled, but didn't speak. She was too busy letting her eyes drift shut as she released a soft "mmm." Then he felt her belly tremble beneath his fingertips, and his dick nearly leaped off the bed in response.

"Keep that up," he growled, "and I won't last long."

She opened her eyes slowly and damned if she didn't look like a queen awakening by slow inches. "Then you'd better get undressed."

He nodded, unable to respond. His fingers fumbled on his tie, but she helped him. And together they got him out of his shirt, as well. Then she pushed his hands away as she bent to undo his belt buckle. He didn't mind, especially as he got quite the view of her behind in the mirror. In fact, he scooted back on the bed just so she would have to lean over more.

She knew what he was doing, of course. And rather than be shocked, she looked up at him, winked and then wiggled her bottom.

Again, he nearly jerked off the bed. But this time she was ready for him. As his hips thrust of their own accord, she took hold and let him push through the circle of her hand and fingers.

"Oh, God, Ali. I don't want this to end too soon."

"Not a problem," she said, as she gave him a squeeze that had his toes curling into the carpet. He didn't remember kicking off his shoes, but at some point he had. Ten seconds later, he thought *to hell with it* and just stripped out of everything.

He sat there naked on the bed while she gave him a tease of a smile. "That is a lovely sight," she said. "And before I forget…"

She slowly spun around on her toe and sashayed her way to her purse. Bending over from the waist, she kept her bottom high as she rooted around in her purse and finally produced a foil-wrapped condom.

"Want me to put it on you?" she asked without straightening.

"I want you to stay right like that," he answered. Then he stood up. Lord, it would be so easy to slip behind her. He wanted to, but he wanted it to last, too. And be good for her.

So while she was still bent over, he stepped near enough to fondle, but not close enough to be tempted where he didn't belong without a condom.

He took his time. He stroked her legs and slid his hands over her delicious ass. Her legs were strong, her bottom tight and high. And then he gently caressed his way up her back to pop her bra.

Then, while she remained frozen in place—except for her excited, breathy pants—he pulled off her bra and began to fondle her breasts.

"I love these," he said as he tweaked and pulled at her nipples. "I love the weight of them in my hands," he said as he cupped and lifted both breasts. "I love the sounds you make as I squeeze them." She was making them now. Soft gasps. Not a moan, not a vocalization at all. Just hitching gasps.

He felt the tension building in her. He wasn't sure how

he knew except that he had made a study of her body as he touched her. His thigh was pressing against hers and he could feel as she relaxed her legs enough to push back against him. She was growing really excited just from breast play, and he loved it.

She held up the condom. "Put it on," she gasped.

"Not yet. I'm not done yet."

She groaned, but in a good way. He stayed with what he was doing for a bit. Then he helped her straighten up even as he slid her panties all the way down. She was wearing strappy sandals that added about three inches to her height. That ought to be about enough, but he wasn't sure.

"Come over here," he said as he pulled her to the full-length mirror. He stood behind her, placing her so she faced the mirror as he stood behind. He could see both excitement and anxiety in her expression, and it took him a moment to realize why.

"Condom," she said, holding it out.

This time he agreed, and she watched as he ripped open the packet and rolled it on. It was cold and not at all what he wanted, but it warmed quickly enough. And it would lead to something much, much better.

Especially as she grinned at him. "Thank you," she whispered.

He frowned a moment. "For putting on a condom?"

She nodded. "Some guys don't like using them."

He looked at her face and guessed that her last boyfriend had been one of "some guys." "Well," he grumbled back, "some guys are assholes."

"Thank God you're not," she said as she reached up to kiss him. She pressed her mouth to his and he took full advantage of it, thrusting into her mouth and toying with her tongue until he was the one who had to break it off. Hell, she made him so hot he was going to explode!

Trying to cool himself off, he broke away and put his naked

backside against the wall. It was cold and really not that comfortable, but that was the point. Meanwhile, he turned her back to his front, facing the mirror.

And there, full-length in front of him, was her body in glorious detail. Full breasts, narrow waist, strong legs and at the juncture of her thighs, that coil of hair that seemed to beckon him.

He looked back up to her eyes in the mirror. He met her gaze and watched as she wet her lips. "What is your fantasy, Ken? What happens now?"

You tell me that you love me.

The words echoed through his thoughts enough to jolt him out of his lust. Holy moly, he hadn't been thinking love. Or at least he didn't want to be thinking love right now. It was too soon. This was a summer promotional tour, for God's sake. He knew that at the end of the summer, the whole tour would feel surreal. As though it had happened in a dream. It was ridiculous to start thinking words like *love* with a woman on a summer tour. Ridiculous, and yet his mind still echoed with the word.

Love.

She must have sensed his fear. She must have known his heart had sped up to near-lethal levels because she turned to look over her shoulder at his face. "Ken? Are you all right?"

He forced himself to nod, and then gently turned her back to the mirror. He could see that his reflection was pale. He could also feel that he was starting to recover as he forced that word out of his brain.

"Let me look at you," he said. And he did. He looked at her breasts as he cupped them again in his hands. He looked at her tight nipples, and he listened to her gasp. He looked at her curls as he slipped his fingers between her legs. And he felt her moisture as he began stroking her there.

By the time she let her head drop back against his shoulder and her legs eased wider, he had nearly forgotten *that* word. Instead, he felt her writhing against him. He heard her keening cries as the tension in her body built. So close, but he didn't want her to finish without him.

So he pulled his hand back and gently nudged her to support her weight. He urged her legs open and pressed her hands forward to frame the mirror. Looking over her shoulder, he had such a vision. Her breasts reflected in front of him. Her narrow waist and then a peek at her curls. Then he helped her adjust her hips as he pushed inside her.

"You feel so great," he groaned. Tight, wet, sweet.

"I was about to say the same thing," she said, her words short and breathy.

He was a little too tall for this and the angle was wrong for full movement, but that was the point.

"Ali—" he began, but then she gripped him with her internal muscles. Tight and hard, and it nearly made his head explode. "Oh, God!" he gasped.

She chuckled and he felt the rhythm of her laughter all the way through his organ and up his spine.

"Ali!" he gasped as she did it again.

She was moving too fast. He was going to come long before she did. And so he did the only thing he could manage. He kept his hips as still as possible so that he wouldn't unseat himself, and then he began to stroke her.

He started with her breasts, but in the end, he had to abandon them as he stroked her cleft. Up and down as she writhed on his pole. He didn't move. *Don't move!*

Her legs were tightening, her head was thrown back. What a sight she was! He stroked her. Faster and harder. And with a free hand, he pinched her nipple.

Again and…

She cried out, her entire body rolling as she came. He wanted to watch. He wanted to just feel what happened as she came apart, but it was too much. Her contractions kicked him over the edge.

He thrust deep, exploding.
And it felt like…
Love.

17

THE WAVE HIT—again—and Ali cried out. They were on her bed, and her head pressed back into her pillow, her pelvis ground hard into Ken's and her legs gripped him as the wave peaked and released, peaked and released.

Damn, they were good at this.

Fantasy sex had been great in front of the mirror. But they hadn't stopped there. They'd started talking as they cuddled close in her bed. And then postsex talk had progressed to caressing, then kissing. And in rather speedy progression, they'd gone on to another mind-blowing orgasm. Lord, she might even have screamed, and she was *not* a screamer. Well, not usually.

Ken collapsed, politely taking his weight onto his arms as he slid sideways. He groaned as he did it, tugging her close as he rolled to his side.

"Best queen ever," he said.

"Best boss ever," she returned.

He groaned. "Don't call me that. Not in bed."

"What if I want to play out my slutty secretary/horny boss fantasy?"

He stilled suddenly and cracked an eye. "Seriously? You have a—" He couldn't even say the words. Fortunately, he looked intrigued, not horrified.

She grinned. "I have a *lot* of fantasies."

"Marry me. We'll pick a different fantasy every night."

Ali didn't answer. The words *marry me* had effectively ended all power of thought or response. Especially since he had said it in jest. It wasn't that she had expected them to get married or anything. But his words blindsided her with their power. She could absolutely see marrying him. And so the idea that he could joke about it—that the idea was funny to him—well, that hurt. And the power of that hurt was what stunned her.

To his credit, he realized that he had screwed up. In truth, he looked as if the words shocked him almost as much as they had surprised her. But he was the one who'd put it out there. And so he was the one scrambling to recover.

"Uh…I mean…I—" He swallowed. "Oh, shit. I know better than to joke about that sort of stuff. I'm so sorry."

She forced a smile and a chuckle that didn't come off so well. "It's fine, Ken. Not a problem. I knew you were joking."

"Um, yeah. I was, but…" He rubbed a hand over his face. "But I brought it up. So let's talk about it."

Panic clutched her chest and she desperately wanted to run away. But they were wrapped together, their legs still intertwined, their faces just inches apart. She couldn't move away without making things ten times more awkward.

So she turned her face into her pillow and faked a big yawn. "It's really late, Ken."

"Don't run from me, Ali. Not now, after I've dropped a bombshell."

She peeked up at him. Nice that he could be so mature about the topic when she was acting like a three-year-old.

"Okay. We'll talk," she said as she forced herself to sit up. She pulled the sheets with her, covering her torso enough to be decent. He shifted to accommodate her, allowing her to pull the covers however she wanted, adjust them however she wanted, *delay* however she wanted. But in the end, she gave in. "So, Ken, what do you want to talk about?"

He gave her a grimace, but nodded. "Okay, here it is. I want to get married someday. I want kids. I want a successful company making a lot of money, and I want that with someone who can laugh with me."

She blinked, startled by his words. "Laugh?"

He nodded. "Yeah. Look, let's be honest, I'm not going to suddenly metamorphosize into a man with movie-star looks."

She smiled. "I think you look just fine. Besides, I'm not going to suddenly look like Michelle Pfeiffer either."

"Thank goodness. Blondes have never been my thing."

"Liar. All guys want blondes with big boobs."

"Yeah, all guys who are fourteen. But then we grow up and become more discriminating." He leaned forward and gave her a kiss. "Believe me when I say you look fine to me." He lengthened the word *fine* so that she felt like he was calling her both beautiful *and* sexy. How cool was that?

She would have deepened the kiss. She would have pulled him closer for another round of fun sex play. But he was being serious, so he pulled back.

"Okay, your turn."

"What?"

"Your hopes and goals and stuff. I told you mine."

"What do I want in a man?" She sighed as she tried to seriously answer the question. She ended up with one thing. "I just want someone who loves me no matter what."

"That's it?"

She shrugged. "Last boyfriend had conditions. He loved me if I cooked for him, cleaned the apartment and generally took total care of him and didn't challenge him too much."

"Loser. Him, not you."

She nodded. "Yeah, and when he dumped me, I was devastated."

He sobered. "I'm sorry, Ali. You deserve so much better."

"I agree. I am not that little girl anymore. I'm a woman who wants marriage and kids someday. With a guy who loves me."

He looked at her a moment, his head cocked to the side as if he were listening to something underneath her words. He probably was because a moment later, he'd accurately read her subtext.

"You mean you've gotten used to expecting so little from life."

She straightened. "Not true! And certainly not anymore." She huffed as she slumped backward. How did she explain this? "This summer has changed me. I'm stronger than I ever was before. I feel bolder, happier." She shot him a coy look. "Sexier."

"That's good."

"No, that's great. For the first time in my life I feel like I can go for what I want. If I can strut around in a corset in front of screaming fans, then I can also look my boss in the eye and demand a raise. I know the two don't exactly correlate—"

"Sure they do."

"But I can do it."

He touched her cheek with his index finger. It was a soft stroke with exquisite tenderness, and she couldn't help but close her eyes to feel every sensation as his finger slid to her lips. When he spoke, it was in a whisper.

"When I was younger and things got hard, I retreated into gaming."

"I read. Book after book after book. I read while I babysat my brothers. I read between classes and at lunch. I even read at my fast-food job when the drive-through lane got slow."

"So way back when, what were your dreams?"

She laughed. "You mean other than being a vampire huntress?"

"Yeah. Let's stick to the nonparanormal right now. Did you want to be a brilliant scientist with a Nobel Prize?"

"I hate science."

"First woman president?"

"Failure at politics. Too shy." Then she smiled in memory. "When I was little, I wanted to be a writer."

"There you go—"

"I tried it. Even had a poem published in a newsletter. But it was too hard and not what I wanted."

"Okay. Well, good. You tried something. It didn't work out, but you tried."

"And I was trying at college, but the money ran out. I ended up at the hospital and I've been there ever since. I'd like to finish school, but don't know in what."

"How about business? Marketing?"

She thought about it. A few years ago, her knee-jerk reaction would be that she wasn't smart enough to run a business or a marketing department. But after working under the head of the hospital PR department, she knew that she could do that job. And if she could run a PR department, what was stopping her from running a whole business?

"What are you thinking?" he pressed.

"I'm thinking that I should believe in myself more. That I should have believed a long time ago but that it took strutting around in a corset for me to see that I can do a lot more than I ever thought."

His eyebrows shot up. "Wow! I thought it would take way more time to get you there."

"I'm shy, not stupid," she said with a laugh. Then she sobered because he was still looking at her with a very serious, steady gaze.

"What would it take, Ali Flores, for you to reach for your dreams? For you to apply all those smarts and focus on something you really want? What would it take?"

The answer came to her quietly and very slowly. It was as if the word had to work its way through all her automatic denials until she heard it in her head. And even then, her heart quailed and her body tried to fight it.

"Ali? What are you thinking?"

That she needed *him*. By her side, pushing her to believe in herself every day for the rest of her life. But she couldn't say that. It would be too bold, especially after his "marry me" mistake. So she opted for something that he would accept. A partial truth, if not a full confession.

"I think I need to make a plan. I'm good at plans."

He nodded. "And?"

She shrugged. "And then I need to carry it out."

He smiled at her. "Have you ever done this before? Have you ever sat down and written out a plan for yourself?"

"Lots of times," she answered. "I've got a plan for how I'm going to pay off my car. How I'm going to get a coffee table. For how I'm going to manage which project at work."

"But nothing for your life. Why?"

"Because," she said, and this time she could see from his face that he wasn't going to accept a partial truth. So she told him it all. "Because then I'd have to do it. And I think I was just too tired to go for it. I've had a job since I was sixteen. I worked in college, too, plus babysitting for my mom because she needed the help. It's only in the last couple years that I've worked at one job and not filled in every waking moment with some other type of work."

"So are you rested? Are you ready to take control again?"

"I am," she said. A quiet excitement started to build inside her as she thought of all the possibilities before her. Suddenly the future was rich with possibilities instead of filled with frightening pitfalls. "After all, that's what this summer was about. Me stepping out of my comfort zone to do something new."

He stroked her face again. This time he used his full palm. "You could do so much, Ali. I can't wait to see where you go."

"Me, too," she whispered. She would make her plan. She would juggle the finances. She would see about a business degree or at least finishing college. And then, look out world! Ali was on her way!

With those thoughts spinning in her mind, she wrapped her arms around his chest. Together, they snuggled down into the sheets.

"You're good for me," she said.

"Well, it's about time someone was."

She smiled as he pressed a kiss to the top of her head. She closed her eyes, her head on his shoulder. And as she drifted off to sleep, she allowed herself to dream the big dream. Not college or even multi-zillionaire business. No, the big dream was being just like this, falling asleep on his shoulder, while they built their awesome future together.

Good thing she knew this was just a summer-tour fling. Otherwise, she might really be tempted to take everything that had just happened much too seriously. She was busy convincing herself of that when Ken's cell phone rang. Five minutes later, Ken was white as a sheet and Ali was driving them both to the hospital.

_18_

KEN RUSHED THROUGH the hospital emergency-room doors with Ali at his side. He quickly scanned the waiting area and found Paul sitting there, unnaturally still as he stared into the depths of a dark cup of coffee. Ken went to his friend's side immediately, but walking across the reception area took a little bit of time. About twenty steps, but it was enough for the pit in Ken's stomach to yawn wider and darker.

Paul wasn't moving. He wasn't making notes, checking his smartphone or doing any of the things that Paul did. He was just sitting motionless. And that meant things were bad. Really bad.

Without even thinking about it, Ken reached for Ali's hand. She was there at his side, her response immediate. And as they made it to Paul, she squeezed his hand for support.

"Hey," Ken said as he settled in the seat beside his best friend.

"Hey," came Paul's lackluster response. Then the man seemed to pull himself together. He took a deep breath and went into what Ken called his executive mode. He summarized the facts—just the facts—in a quick and brutal fashion. "Tina was…was doing something with the costumes. I don't even know what. Had to get them patched or something, but she took a cab. She was on the way back to the hotel when it happened. The cab got hit by another car. T-boned. Cabdriver was killed instantly. Other driver soon after."

"Oh, no," whispered Ali. This time it was Ken who squeezed her hand.

"Tina's alive, but she's beaten up pretty bad. She's headed for surgery."

"Surgery?" Ken asked.

Paul nodded. "Her legs are real bad. They've got to pin them and stuff. I…um…I wrote down all the details." He fumbled in his pocket and came out with a crumpled napkin. He held it out, and Ali took it from Paul's shaking hand.

Ali was the one who opened it up and showed it to him. The list was pretty extensive, but it all looked fixable. Assuming a shattered tibia and fibula were fixable.

"Is she in a lot of pain?" Ali asked.

Paul nodded and if possible, he went even more pale. "They doped her up pretty good, but she was screaming." He took a shuddering breath. "I was the contact person she gave to the paramedics. They called me on her cell phone and I could hear her screaming in the background. I could hear it."

Oh. Wow. Tina was not a screamer. Not a pain-screamer, that is. He didn't know about the rest. And his mind was just circling on stupidities because he couldn't process the rest. Tina. Car accident. Surgery.

"She'll be fine," Ken said to himself as much as to Paul.

Paul nodded. "She's a fighter."

"She's amazing," Ali said. "At everything. And that means she's strong. She'll pull through this." She held up the list. "Paul, none of this is life-threatening. Horrible. Going to keep her off stilettos for a while. But she'll pull through just fine."

Paul looked up, his heart in his eyes. "I know. I just keep thinking what if—"

"Don't go there!" Ali's voice was strong. Like superhero-strong. She had the ring of command and both Paul and Ken immediately responded to the tone. They straightened in their seats and looked at her. Meanwhile, she kept her eyes level and her voice calm. "She's alive and going to get better. I'm going to talk to the nurse over there and figure out what we can do. What's going on. You guys just sit here. I'll be right back." Then she glanced at Ken. "Do you want any coffee or anything?"

Ken flashed her a grateful smile. "No. I'm good, but thanks. And, um, thanks for…" He gestured toward the nurse and the crumpled napkin in Ali's hand.

"No problem," she answered. Then she put her hand on Paul's shoulder a moment before turning and heading toward the reception area.

"Hell," said Paul. Nothing more. Just hell.

Ken nodded. "Yeah."

ALI HAD NEVER SEEN Paul look so awful. In fact, she couldn't remember a time she'd seen him *not* moving, not smiling, not…anything. It was startling and made her wonder if there was more to Paul and Tina than anybody knew.

Her gaze traveled to Ken who was a rock of moral support. But he was also a guy, so that meant he sat there looking awkward and glancing at her. He was also surreptitiously making notes on a pad that appeared from somewhere. For all she knew, it was Paul's and Ken had just commandeered it.

Either way, she knew what he was doing. After all, he couldn't help Tina or Paul, except to sit there in case someone needed something. But he could make sure that all of Tina's hard work didn't go to waste. He was making lists of things that would have to be handled. Truthfully, she was, too. And between the two of them—plus a brilliant medical staff—she was sure everything would work out.

Ken looked up at her, and she smiled encouragingly at him. Tina was in surgery, the dawn was creeping over the city and soon the rest of the troupe was going to appear with their bags packed wondering where the two bosses were. She would have to figure out what they were going to do soon. The schedule was packed pretty tight. They couldn't afford to stay here.

She pulled out a water bottle from the vending machine and brought it over to Paul, forcibly putting it in his hands.

"Hydrate," she ordered.

He blinked, focused on her, then obeyed. After taking a few obligatory sips, he focused on his surroundings, his eyes narrowing as he looked out the window.

"It's morning."

Ken nodded. "I know."

"We're supposed to be leaving soon. We can't miss those dates. We need them. The sales—"

Ken squeezed his friend's arm. "I know, Paul. I know."

"But—"

"I can drive us," Ali interrupted. "I can drive the bus."

Both men cut their gazes to her. "You can? It's not the same as a car, you know. We had to take special classes and practice. A lot." That was Ken, his head tilted slightly, but his expression was hopeful. He, Paul and Tina were the three who had been driving the bus.

Ali grimaced. "Okay, *I* can't drive the bus, but I was checking on the internet. We can hire a bus driver. It shouldn't be too expensive."

"Great idea," said Ken. "Do it."

Paul grimaced. "You should go, too. You can do some of the driving."

Ken shook his head. "I'm not leaving."

"Don't be ridiculous—"

"Tina's my friend, too. I'm not letting her wake up alone in a strange hospital in a strange city."

Paul nodded slowly, his gaze slipping back toward the surgical wing. "She's got family. We need to call them."

Ali cleared her throat, feeling awkward, but knowing they needed someone to handle these things right then. "I've got her cell phone and her planner. The hospital got them from the police. All the information is there. I'm just waiting until a little later in the morning to start calling."

Paul frowned. "You got her planner?"

She nodded, but she didn't want to show it to him. There was blood on it. "Yeah. She kept everything in there."

"Not everything. Her laptop's in her hotel room. I think."

"Good. I'll check on that." Then Ali bit her lip. "If I could make a suggestion?" She looked at both Paul and Ken.

"Please," said Ken. "I'd love a suggestion."

"I know this might look opportunistic—"

"Ali, we know you're trying to help." That was Paul, his expression rueful. "It's not like I'm functioning on all cylinders right now. Whatever you can do is very welcome."

Meanwhile, Ken flashed a very brief smile at her. "How about I preempt the awkwardness here? Ali, how would you like a job? Just a temporary one until Tina can come back, but we need someone to take over the logistics here. I'll pay you what Tina makes—"

"We don't need to talk pay now."

"The hell we don't. You'll get what Tina gets."

She nodded, knowing that she was going to earn every penny. "Then I accept with gratitude. Now here's what we're going to do…" She pulled out her list. Ken pulled out his. And even Paul managed to find his iPad.

Five exhausting hours later, the bus was on the road with a new driver, she'd made her calls to Tina's family and helped them get flights, and she'd even figured out Tina's to-do list before the next event. Fortunately, Tina was almost as organized as Ali was. Unfortunately, taking her list plus Ken's and Paul's to-do lists was like trying to move three mountains all at once. But she didn't have much choice.

With that thought in mind, she abruptly stood up, balancing herself in the aisle since the bus was moving at a fast clip down the freeway. "Everybody, can I have your attention, please?"

Everyone quieted.

"Okay, so we've suffered a loss. A big one, but it's not fatal—to us or to Tina—thank God. But we're all going to have to pull together to make sure that the show goes on. So here's the deal. I've got about a zillion tasks that need to be done. I'm going to start reading them off. I suggest you volunteer to help because if you don't, I'm going to assign you something. And I can be very evil in assigning tasks. Understand?"

Every person nodded gravely.

She grinned. "Good. All right, task number one..."

KEN COLLAPSED INTO his hotel bed, his eyes gritty, his body aching from exhaustion. Tina was out of surgery, out of recovery and into a room of her own. Both Paul and Ken had been there when she woke up, but Paul was the one who had done all the talking. And his first words had stunned everyone.

He'd said he loved her. Paul loved Tina and wanted to marry her. That's why he'd been so distracted all tour, that's why he'd been screwing up left and right. Because his mind had been filled with Tina and the accident had given him a much-needed wake-up call. He loved her; he wanted to marry her.

Tina had said yes. Then she'd started crying—happy tears—between other equally loving words. So Ken had quietly left the room while his mind and his gut had churned. Paul and Tina were in love. And their happiness had him thinking of Ali. Was it possible for them, too? Or was the end of the tour going to end their relationship, as usually happened with these summer relationships?

Two hours later, Ken left the hospital. He'd stayed long enough to see that Tina was on the mend. The doctor said everything looked good. And since Paul was staying with her—currently sprawled in one of those awful hospital-room chairs—Ken had come back here to collapse on his bed.

All he wanted was to sleep, but he could not sink into oblivion. His bed was too empty and his mind too full. He'd already called Ali a dozen or more times for updates and the like. He knew he was interfering. Worse, he knew he was just wasting her time because she had enough things on her to-do list and not a one of them was chatting on the phone with him.

But he liked talking to her. He missed the sound of her voice and the feel of her body alongside his. And God, he wanted to curl into her side right now and smell her sweet scent. It wasn't a sexual need. He was too exhausted for that. He just wanted her by his side.

Ten minutes later, he was up and packing. Paul had everything under control here. Tina was going to be fine. Ken needed to be with the troupe. More specifically, he needed to be with Ali. So he called the airport, booked a flight and only winced once at the price.

He wouldn't arrive until midnight at the earliest, but he had to get there. He tried to convince himself that he would let her sleep. He tried to believe that he would get his own room and then he'd see her in the morning.

He failed. He knew that he was a weak man when it came to Ali, and he would find a way to get into her bedroom. Whatever time it was, he was going to slip into her bed if only to feel the heat of her again.

The thought terrified him. He really didn't want to need her so much. But he did, and right now, he was too tired to fight the draw. So he packed up and hailed a cab. And just before he boarded the flight, he texted her.

Catching a flight. Be there around 12:30.

He waited a long time before she answered, but when it came, he exhaled a great big sigh of relief.

My room is 824. Key will be at the front desk. If you want.

He grinned. He loved it when a woman read his mind. His text back to her was short and sweet.

I want you.

19

YES, YES!

Ali felt her eyes roll back as ecstasy pulsed through her body. She lived it, she relished it, she loved it…and then it faded. Ken collapsed sideways, his own orgasm leaving him spent and happy. She could tell because he was grinning. And even as he fell to the side completely boneless, his hands always sought hers. Her fingers, her palms, or whatever part of her was closest. He would touch her, absently rub his thumb across her skin, and he would grin.

They had been together every night for weeks now. Though they tried to keep their relationship low-key, everyone in the troupe knew. Fortunately, beyond a few teasing comments, no one had a particular problem with it. No one, that is, except for Blake who gave her long, puppy-dog-sad looks every now and then. She laughed them off, as did he, but inside she felt awkward and embarrassed. She was doing the boss. Every night. That was awkward.

And it was also increasingly sad. Because she felt the end of the summer coming like a big guillotine on their relationship. Sure they lived in the same city, but Houston wasn't exactly small. And besides, as everyone on staff had told her over and over, she should not expect this summer out of time to be anything but that: a summer fling. Everything changed once people got home. Best friends drifted apart. Romances ended—always. Some bitterly, some slowly, but they always ended.

The romantic in her wanted to believe that she and Ken were different. But her practical side said two words: *fat chance.* Summer flings didn't last past the first autumn leaf.

So she guarded her heart. She filled her days with work—doing her job plus Tina's was keeping her excruciatingly busy—and at night she and Ken explored all sorts of fun stuff. But every moment of every day, she had to remind herself that it wasn't going to last beyond October first.

They were on the last big stop before the end of the tour. It was Labor Day weekend at DragonCon, a fantasy/science-fiction convention with eighty thousand people. The event took over five hotels in downtown Atlanta, and was something that would have overwhelmed her at the beginning of the summer. Not so now.

Now, thanks to a summer of practice and the way Ken's eyes lit up every time she strutted into the booth, she had the confidence to act like a queen. Now she knew that the people—kids and adults—who came to hang out around her just wanted her to listen to them. She said almost nothing at all about the product, but they still bought. They just needed a friend.

In short, she had to realize being a queen had absolutely nothing to do with her as a person. She was simply a listener. And in listening, she had met all sorts of fantastic people.

Now it was time for the main event. The whole summer had been building to the big showdown between Arthur and Lancelot. Who would defeat the other in battle? Who would win Queen Guinevere's heart? And, in a marked departure from the traditional Arthurian legend, Ali didn't hide in the background on this one. For DragonCon, she was coming out in her Warrior Queen outfit complete with leather boots, short sword and *attitude.*

Looking back at the summer, Ali couldn't believe the changes in herself. Her first event had had her nauseous with anxiety. Today, she was actually excited to go on stage and kick some butt. But there were more changes, too. She'd been looking for something different for the summer. What she found instead was herself—different shades, different flavors, but all of them strong. She discovered that Sexy Ali was fun, Marketing Ali was good, but *Managerial* Ali was where she totally rocked. And that didn't even begin to address In Love Ali, but she wasn't going to think about that. Not with the end of the summer perilously close.

She was waiting behind the stage when Paul joined her. After Tina's accident, he had spent five days by her side. But then he'd returned to the troupe, and except for daily texts and calls, he acted as if nothing had changed. Except, of course, Ali had heard from Ken that he and Tina were engaged. The two kept it quiet for their own reasons, but every time Ali looked at Paul, she saw the happiness that simmered right behind his eyes. The man was in love, and that made all the difference.

"Hey, Paul," she said when he came up beside her. "Everything okay?"

He nodded. "Everything's fine, but…you know how we've been building to today? The whole tour has been set to reveal who wins you today. Do you go with Lancelot or Arthur?"

She knew. And all the blogs, web surveys and player input had been for Lancelot. By an overwhelming margin. So that was the plan for today. She was going to strut into the middle of the battle, declare that no one could pick her man for her and then choose the warrior everyone wanted her to pick. Which, sadly, was Lancelot. Blake's blond good looks plus that blog about their "date" had really turned the tide of public opinion his way.

"Yeah, I know," she said. "I'll drag it out, but in the end, it's gotta be Lancelot."

Paul grimaced and looked acutely uncomfortable. "It doesn't have go that way, you know," he finally said. "Just answer with your heart."

Ali frowned, not understanding what he was saying. Answer with her heart? This was a promotional tour. The fans wanted Lancelot and Guinevere to finally have their day. "But—" she began, but he just grabbed her hand and drew her closer to him. It would be almost romantic if it weren't so weird. "Paul—"

He kissed her on the cheek. "I'm not even supposed to be talking to you. Just, you know, answer honestly. That's the best anyone can do."

Then before she could say more, he just gave her a thumbs-up and hurried away. She would have followed. She hated surprises and damn if she was going to let a conversation like that just hang there. But then the music started and he jumped up on stage. Mordred was opening today's event, laughing and gloating over the war in the kingdom.

Meanwhile, Ali stood in the wings replaying the conversation in her mind. None of it made sense.

She waited, listening with half an ear as the battle scene began. Clash of swords, roar of the crowd, all the usual stuff. She peeked through and saw that both Blake and Ken were going all-out. She didn't really care what Blake looked like, but she saw Ken, his royal robe billowing behind him as he fought, his sword sweeping through the air. Good God, he looked amazing. Muscles, sword, cape—how could anyone look at Blake when Ken was there?

She was just about to go on stage when suddenly, Ken put on a burst of speed. Usually Blake was the better sword fighter. After all, he was younger and when he wasn't messing with his hair, he was working out. But this time, Ken was the greater one by far. Blow after blow after blow he beat Lancelot back. It was like Ken/King Arthur was possessed, and Ali couldn't take her eyes off him. She was supposed to step on stage and stop the battle, but she was so entranced by his victory, she couldn't move.

Then Lancelot tripped and Ken pinned him with his knee. The crowd was going wild, but not in support for Arthur. They wanted Lancelot to win, and this defeat in battle didn't sit well with them. Broken from her trance, Ali rushed on stage.

Except for her crown, she was dressed all in leather. Corset and boots and very little else meant the crowd's attention was riveted on her. She slowed just enough to remember to put some swagger into her strut and she went center stage. Ken was still there, his knee pinning Blake to the floor. And as Ali came up, she couldn't resist touching the sleek bulge of his biceps. Over the past month, she'd touched every part of his body. She'd kissed and caressed and a whole more, but this moment was special. He was special, and she looked at him with her heart in her eyes.

If only this summer could go on forever. If only they could live in this fantasy Camelot forever. But they couldn't. And she had a job to do.

So she stepped back and said her lines. "What foolishness is this? What makes you think a sword can win me or my favors?"

The crowd roared. There were at least as many women in the audience as men, and that statement was a real pleaser to the female set.

The swords came down. Blake's didn't have far to go since he was already on the ground. Meanwhile, Ken straightened and bowed before his queen.

"Of course," he said in his most regal tone. "My lady, I would speak with you."

Then Blake, mindful of his position as hero, also leaped up and bowed before her. "I, too, my queen, would beg an audience."

Ali nodded, stepping backward enough to allow the men the room on stage. Blake went first, going through his scripted lines of adoration. He loved her, he wanted her, blah, blah, blah. Ali knew the words and barely listened, especially since he seemed to be speaking more to the crowd than to her, though the audience, of course, was eating it up because Blake was actually a very good actor.

Then it was Ken's turn. "My Guinevere," he said, his voice pitched for everyone but his eyes on hers. "I have learned so much in my travels to this moment in time. I have laughed at the strangest times and found joy in places I never thought to look. I have discovered a value in silence and looked beneath the surface of your still pond and discovered such wonder."

He spoke the words with such passion, such power, even when he stumbled slightly over the word *pond*. And he kept speaking, though Ali could barely hear it over the roaring in her ears. He looked so earnest. If it weren't for the costumes and the crowd, she could imagine him trying to propose to her this way. And the sight hurt. It hurt because it wasn't real.

Meanwhile, he kept speaking, his words unrelentingly earnest. "Guinevere, you are everything to me. My day cannot begin except that I see you. Sleep will not come unless I cradle you close. No moment, no summer, no life, would be complete unless you are part of it."

He stopped speaking, and she just looked at him. Her eyes were watering, her belly was tight and her mouth was hideously dry. She had no idea what she was supposed to do now. How did this relate to the game? What was he doing? She didn't know, and the whole thing was too painful on every level. Her only urge was to run, but she couldn't. She was supposed to stay on stage.

"And so, my queen…" Ken reached into a hidden pocket beneath his breeches and pulled out a diamond ring. It had to be cubic zirconia because it was really large. And it sparkled under the stage lights. "Will you do me the greatest honor a man can have and become my wife? Um…again?"

She stared at the ring and then up at Ken. She couldn't tell.

Was this a proposal, as in a *real* proposal? It couldn't be. And yet it felt real. She looked out at the crowd, seeing the misty-eyed looks of some of the women. They were eating this up.

So did that mean this was a publicity stunt? A last ramp-up of the struggle between Arthur and Lancelot for her affection? She didn't know and her head was swimming with the possibilities.

She took a shuddering breath, struggling for some understanding. In the end, she fell back on the script. When all else failed, this was about selling a computer game. So she looked out at the crowd, pitching her voice to carry.

"Ladies, gentlemen, what should I do? Who is most worthy of my gifts and my love?"

The response was deafening, and the opinion was split. So she did what they'd been doing all summer. She looked out at the crowd and she asked them to vote. How did they vote? With their dollars. They played the game on the side of either Lancelot or Arthur, and then the game told them who had won her heart based on their score.

The crowd didn't like that. They wanted a winner and a loser. But Ali couldn't decide. Not until she knew if that had been a real proposal or a game one. And that's when Paul stepped in. He was Mordred, so he came on sneering and laughing, pushing the crowd to demand she choose.

So she did. She picked Lancelot because that's what the online players had demanded. With tears in her eyes, she rushed to Blake. She said the words she'd memorized and Lancelot was declared the winner. And as soon as she could possibly manage, she got off the stage and ran to her room.

KEN STARED AT THE SPOT where Ali was supposed to be. He stared at it, his knee throbbing and his heart in his belly.

She'd said no. He'd worked for a week on his lines, he'd bought the largest diamond he could afford, and he'd endured an agony of nerves as he prepared to bare his soul in front of a few thousand people.

He'd done all of that, and she'd said no. She'd asked the crowd what she should do and then let them force her to pick Blake. Then she'd run off stage.

The crowd was beginning to titter. What the hell had he been thinking to propose to a woman in so public a way? He'd been thinking about his female friends. He'd been thinking about his half sister who used to go on and on about how she wanted a proposal with a zillion witnesses. One that would be replayed on YouTube. That would be talked about with envy by all her friends. That's what he'd been thinking, and here he was, on his knee, while behind him a thousand strangers laughed at him.

He felt his face burn with embarrassment. And not just his face but his whole body—which was neatly exposed for everyone to see. Oh, God.

Thankfully, this was the last major stop on the tour. As the loser, King Arthur was supposed to disappear. It had always been part of the plan that he would leave after DragonCon. It was one of the reasons he proposed today because if Ali said yes, he would remain with her for the last couple of dates.

But she hadn't, and he couldn't face her. He just…couldn't.

So he put on a shirt, gave the sword to Paul because it wouldn't go through security and hopped a cab for the airport.

_20_

IT TOOK TWO HOURS before Ali realized her mistake. She'd left the main stage and headed straight to her room where she'd stripped out of all her "queen" clothes, showered off all the makeup and sweat and then put on jeans and a T-shirt. Finally, she felt exactly like herself!

Except, of course, she'd been dieting, so the jeans hung baggily. She'd also spent the summer getting used to a corset, so her T-shirt felt like a tent. Sure she could breathe easily, but her back felt unsupported.

It didn't matter. For this moment in time, she had ditched corsets and queens, geeks and freaks, and everything in between. And she had certainly, positively, had it with actors and Arthur!

Of course the Arthur in question would likely be coming in the door any second now. The show was definitely over. There would be cleanup and sales stuff to handle, but she had no doubt he would be headed her way soon. Part of her welcomed it. She wanted to have it out with him. Really express exactly what she felt in the privacy of their hotel room. And there was a measure of how much she'd grown over the summer because, frankly, this was exactly the type of conversation she would normally have run screaming from.

Was that a real proposal or not? Did he want to marry her?

Or was that a last-ditch publicity stunt to ramp up sales for "Team Arthur"?

And then, of course, was the really awful question: Did *she* want to marry *him?* Well, of course she did. She was in love with him, after all. But once again, this was a summer of fantasy and everyone had been telling her to not put faith in a summer romance.

Oh, hell. What did she want? To wait, obviously. Until the summer was over and she had some perspective. To see if he was going to dump her as soon as the next tour came along. Or a week after returning to Houston.

She heard footsteps coming down the hallway and held her breath in panic. Was that Ken? Apparently not, because whoever it was kept on going right past the room. Well, clearly she couldn't stay here. So with sudden resolve, she grabbed her purse and rushed out of the room. But where could she go?

The art room. She liked art, right? And she'd wanted to see the incredible display of beauty and whimsy that was part of fantasy art. She headed there as fast as the elevators, walkways and escalators could get her there.

And that's where Samantha found her an hour later. Ali was pretending to be enthralled by paintings of kittens with wings. It wasn't so much the little kittens that intrigued her. They were cute and all, like furry cherubs. But she'd been caught by an image of a fierce adult cat—a lioness—with her wings cut backward as she leaped to attack a hapless gazelle. It was fierce and bold and she was caught by the beauty of a creature so lethal.

"Thinking of killing Ken?" Samantha asked.

Ali started, turning to smile at Sam. "What? Oh, no. Well, maybe."

"Look, I'm not going to belabor this. If you want to talk, I'm here. But there's something I think you need to know."

Ali nodded, bracing herself inside. She could tell by the

set of Sam's face that she wasn't going to like whatever was coming next. "Okay. Hit me."

"I won't go into the stupidity of proposing to a woman like you while in costume in front of thousands of screaming fans. Or how dumb it is to completely spring something like that on anyone."

"So it was a real proposal?" Ali asked, feeling her gut roil.

"He thought he was being romantic. Which just goes to show how stupid these guys can be sometimes."

"Romantic?" Ali asked.

"Like the guys on TV. And YouTube and everywhere else."

"So, not a publicity stunt?"

"Nope."

Ali just stared at her. The words simply didn't compute. Sure they'd talked about marriage. Eventually. Someday. But she'd refused to think beyond the end of the summer. But apparently Ken had. Ken had been thinking very much beyond their last tour stop next week.

And while she stood there with her mouth hanging open, Samantha released a sigh. "Come on. Let's get something to eat. There's a cheap Chinese place around the block. I'm dying for some crab rangoon."

Ali nodded dully. Her mind had just stuttered to a stop. Ken had proposed to her. And she hadn't even known it was a real proposal.

They made it to the restaurant quickly enough. One glance inside told Ali that they would fit right in with the other customers. There was a table of Klingons, another of trolls and three with a mixed bag of zombies, fairies and kilted warriors. At least the robot had taken off most of his costume so that he could eat, which meant that someone else besides her wore a T-shirt, though his had a picture of a depressed Stormtrooper holding his head in his hands and the caption: REGRETS: Those were the droids you were looking for.

She and Sam didn't speak at all as they got their food from

the buffet and dug in. It was the end of the tour so all diets were at an end. Except for Blake, apparently, whose agent had hinted about something big but wouldn't say what.

Finally, after four crab rangoons and a pile of sweet-and-sour chicken, Ali felt strong enough to face the truth.

"Tell me again slowly," she said. "What do you mean that was a real…you know." She couldn't even say the word out loud.

Sam didn't even hesitate. "It was a real diamond, a real proposal. Ken was asking you—for real—to marry him."

Ali shook her head. "He couldn't have. He wouldn't. Haven't you guys spent the last month telling me this affair wasn't serious. That it—"

"Yeah," Sam said as she dropped her fork and leaned back in her chair. "See, we kept thinking he was one of us. You know, an actor. Summer gigs like this, lots of us have affairs. And we learn early not to put our hearts into summer tours."

Ali nodded. That's what every single one of the troupe had said to her either overtly or subtly for the past four weeks.

"The thing is," Sam said as she leaned forward, "we forgot that Ken's not one of us. At his core, he's a geek. He collects comic books, he has a couple of action figures on his desk, and he's got a regular online Dungeons & Dragons group from when he was a kid. He got one of his designers to put the game up online so they could all play from different parts of the country."

Ali knew that. At least those details. But she couldn't understand how Sam got from geek to proposal.

"You don't get it, do you?" Sam asked.

"No."

"In his mind, you've been engaged, married and have a couple kids by now. Ken isn't like Blake or Paul or any of the other guys you're thinking of. He hasn't dated girl after girl since the moment he hit puberty. In fact, I doubt you've seen any pictures of Ken in high school, have you?"

Ali thought back. "No, I haven't. But we've been on tour. It's not like he brought them along on the bus."

"He doesn't bring them anywhere. He didn't start working out until he was in his twenties. And even then, it's not like he can compare with Blake or even Paul. He just hasn't got the physique."

"So? I don't care about that. I never have."

"But don't you see? I don't know that he ever really dated in high school. He was a geek, through and through. So no matter that he owns his own company now, he's still got the geek I'll-never-get-a-woman mindset."

Ali took a deep breath, slowly processing everything Sam was saying. How could she have so misread the man she'd been sleeping with all summer? "You're saying that when we started dating, he was thinking marriage from—"

"The first moment you slept together. Probably the first time you kissed."

Ali looked down at her plate. "He's never spoken about love. Neither have I."

"He did in his proposal."

Ali thought back. "Um, no. Actually, he didn't."

Samantha frowned. "God, he is an idiot."

Ali might have agreed, except she'd just received a proposal of marriage and hadn't even realized it. In the grand scheme of things, that put her as the bigger idiot. With sudden resolve, she pushed back from the table. "I've got to go talk to him."

"You can't. He's gone."

Ali froze before she could take a step away from the table. "What do you mean, he's gone?"

"Paul told me. Ken left for the airport right after the show. Didn't pack a bag or anything. Just hopped a cab and was gone. Paul didn't even try to talk him out of it."

"What?" Ali gasped. Sure she understood—or was beginning to realize—the depth of how humiliated the man was.

After all, he'd just been refused in front of a zillion people. "But to just leave without talking to me…"

Samantha shrugged. "Yeah, I chewed Paul out for letting him go."

Ali shook her head. "When Ken is determined, there's nothing that Paul could say to change his mind."

"Yeah, that's exactly what Paul said."

"Which means he was very determined." And very hurt. Hurt, embarrassed and…heartbroken? The idea was so difficult to process. It had been real. All of it was real.

"Why wouldn't he stay and talk to me?" Even as she asked the question, she knew the answer. It was the same reason she'd fled the stage as soon as she could. It was the same instinct she had to run and hide the second things got too painful. The only difference was that she couldn't go back to Houston. If she'd had the means, she probably would have. Straight back to a pint of chocolate-fudge ice cream and a weepy movie sob-fest with Elisa.

"Besides," said Sam, "wasn't he planning on leaving tomorrow anyway? Wasn't that the schedule?"

Ali nodded as she collapsed back into her seat. "Yeah, that was the schedule." She'd seen it. She'd obsessed about it. She'd even tried to ignore the guillotine-like snick she felt every time she looked at the date. But she hadn't expected that their last night together would be…well, not.

She dropped her head into her hands. "What the hell am I supposed to do now?"

Sam touched her hand then ordered them both chocolate-chip ice cream. And after the bowls came and they both dug in, she finally answered.

"Personally, I'd bury myself in ice cream, then go back to work as if nothing happened."

Ali nodded, thinking that wasn't a bad plan.

"But," Sam continued, "you're not an actor any more than

Ken is. This summer has been about you changing things up, right?"

Ali nodded. "Yeah. You know, coming out of my shell, finding my outer beauty, and…hell, I don't know. It was mostly about just doing something different."

"Okay, so do you feel like a changed woman now?"

Ali shrugged. "I thought so. But some things will never change. I'll never relish the spotlight like you and Blake do."

"That's okay. There are enough of us out there. We don't need more competition."

Ali smiled. "No one can compete with you when you step on the stage."

"Well, maybe, but we were talking about you. So do you feel stronger, bolder, more I-am-woman, hear-me-roar?"

"Definitely."

"And what does Strong Ali think you should do?"

Ali dug out another bite of ice cream and stuffed it into her mouth. "I'll never get over how you actors can just split yourself into multiple personalities."

"Stop avoiding," Sam returned after she'd swallowed her own big bite. "What does the new strong you think you should do?"

"Have it out with Ken. If he really was thinking marriage—"

"Did you see the size of that rock?"

Ali flinched. Yeah, that had been a huge rock. "Okay, if he's thinking of marriage, then we've got to have a talk. We've got to talk about a *lot* of things."

Sam nodded, but her expression was pensive. "I suppose you could go that way. Talk. And more talk."

"And what would you suggest?"

"Me? I'd show up in a trench coat and nothing else. Then do him on his desk."

Ali laughed. "You would not!"

"Of course I would. And then when he was naked and vulnerable, that's when I'd force him to talk."

"Guys aren't usually so coherent at that point in time."

"Exactly! Because when I say talk, I usually mean, I talk and they listen."

Ali wasn't sure guys could handle listening at that point either, but she wasn't about to argue the image. Or that the men would have incentive to pay attention. But even after a summer of sexual exploration, she wasn't about to do that. It was too easy an out for her. In her mind, fantasy sex was fun, but it wasn't real life. And a marriage was built in real life, not bump and grind on a desk. Though there was definite appeal in the idea. Definite appeal.

Sam slowed eating long enough to look at Ali with narrowed eyes. "You're going to do the responsible thing, aren't you?"

Ali grimaced. "I don't know about responsible. I'm going to finish out the tour—"

"Because you're not one to skip out on your commitments."

"And I think I'll email him that I had no idea that it had been a real proposal."

"That'll be a hard thing for him to read."

Not a picnic to write either. But he had to know that she'd been confused. "I'll...uh...I'll tell him that when the tour is over, we should get together and talk."

"Oh, kiss of death."

Ali shook her head. "I'm not trying to be mean. But if he wants a white picket fence and children with me, then we've got to be able to talk like normal people."

Samantha rolled her eyes. "Geeks are *not* normal people."

"They're not space aliens either. We've got to meet halfway at least."

Samantha gave a fatalistic shrug. "Beats me. I'm an actress. I'm more comfortable around space aliens. At least these kinds." She gestured over to a group of guys dressed as aliens who were just now sitting down at a nearby table. And every single one of them was looking at her. "I bet I could get them to pay for our meal if I talked nice to them."

Ali laughed. "I bet you could. But this meal's on me. Which leaves you free to do whatever you want with the aliens."

"You could join me. Get a little geek compare and contrast."

Ali grinned but shook her head. "Sorry, no. I've got more than I can handle with just the one."

And with that she paid the bill and left. She had an email confession to write and absolutely no idea what to say.

21

KEN STARED AT a very nicely and calmly written email and tried not to choke. Only he could manage to propose to a woman and have her not even realize that he was asking her to marry him. God, he was such an idiot.

He read the email again. It was his hundredth time, and he still had no idea how he should respond. Ali's tone was calm, almost professional. There was no sign of emotion or desperate passion anywhere. It was simply an apology and a desire to speak again when the tour was over.

Translation: kiss off, loser.

He read it again trying as best as he could to not *feel* as he read. To look at it as if he were someone completely neutral reading the email. It took him three tries, and in the end he gave up.

The email was too neutral. For a woman who had done the things they'd done in bed, every word here was cool and dispassionate. But maybe it wasn't quite a kiss-off. Then again…

Hell, his mind was going in circles. And truthfully, it didn't matter what she'd written or how. There was a clear invitation to talk and Ken was too much of a masochist not to agree. Plus, he was too much in love with her *not* to grasp at straws. So if dinner and awkward conversation was the straw at hand, he would grab on to it and hold tight.

He typed back a quick email saying he would love to see her. Then he suggested the most expensive restaurant he knew—the kind of place he'd meant to take her on their first date—and added a day and time. Five minutes later, she accepted his offer in two quick sentences:

That sounds lovely. I'll meet you there.

ALI STEPPED INTO THE ELEVATOR that would take her up to the restaurant and hit the button, doing her best not to totter on her heels. She'd spent the summer strutting about in three-inch boots and the like, but now in a normal dress and heels, she felt completely off balance. Or maybe it was *who* she was about to see that had her off-kilter. Either way there was no turning back now.

The elevator dinged, the doors opened and Ali had to restrain a gasp of surprise. Talk about expensive! This was probably the ritziest restaurant she'd ever been to. Oh, hell. She'd planned to pay for her own dinner, if she and Ken politely went their own ways. But looking around, she doubted she could afford what even a salad at this place cost. Especially since she'd decided to quit her job and go to school full-time to finish her college degree. It would only take a year and if she filled in with a part-time job somewhere, she could manage it. But not if she blew her rent on a dinner at this restaurant.

"Good evening, miss," greeted the maître d'. He looked just like a man in his position should look, black tux and all. She flashed on her first date with Ken in Chicago. She doubted this man would burst into a rendition of "YMCA."

She repressed a hysterical giggle at the memory and stepped up to the podium. "H-hello," she finally managed. "I'm—"

"Are you perhaps Miss Flores? Here to dine with Mr. Johnson?"

Ali blinked. Of course a host at a place like this would know her name. They made a point of doing stuff like that. "Um, yes. That's—er, yes, I'm Alicia Flores."

"Then I believe—" he reached over to a nearby table and picked up a long florist's box, opening it with a flourish "—these are for you."

Ali gasped. They were roses. A dozen long-stemmed red roses. She looked, but there wasn't a card. Obviously they were from Ken, but…well, she just didn't know what to think.

"They're beautiful," she murmured.

"Shall I put them in water for you?"

"Oh…of course. Thank you."

He bowed and handed off the box to a waiting busboy. Ali was watching the box disappear when the maître d' turned back to her. "Mr. Johnson called to say that he has been unavoidably detained. This wretched traffic, you know."

"Wretched," Ali echoed because the man seemed to expect it. She hadn't really encountered any terrible pileups or anything, but Ken was likely coming from a different direction.

"Mr. Johnson hopes that you will order whatever appetizer pleases you, and as an added apology, we would like to offer you a complimentary glass of wine."

"Oh. Um, okay." What did one say when a restaurant apologized for one's date being late? "Thank you."

"Our pleasure, Miss Flores. If you would follow me?"

She did, trying not to fall flat on her face. The place was elegant, subdued and had what felt like half a dozen waiters and busboys prepared to meet her every need. There were a few fellow diners, all dressed in suits or sleek dresses. The amount of jewelry that sparkled in the candlelight was practically blinding. Her booth sported a pristine white tablecloth, classic table settings and her roses already artfully arranged.

And once again, she had to restrain an inappropriate giggle. Somehow she'd left the real world and stepped onto the set of a mobster movie or a spy thriller. She half expected

James Bond to appear at the bar and order a martini—shaken, not stirred.

She pulled it together and managed to slide into the booth. Her light sundress was chilly in the air-conditioning, especially since the day happened to be overcast and cool for late September. She shivered.

"I see you're a bit chilled. May I suggest a glass of wine and a lovely loaner shawl that should complement your dress perfectly."

She nodded numbly. What type of restaurant had loaner shawls? Apparently this one. "Thank you," she pushed out through her tight throat. "Red wine, please. Whatever you recommend and, um, the shawl would be welcome."

He bowed. "An excellent selection. And may I recommend the foie gras, as well? It is today's special appetizer, prepared with mustard seeds and green onion in duck jus."

Ali had no idea what all that was, but she hadn't the wherewithal to disagree. So she smiled and nodded, all the while wondering where Ken was. Was it possible? she wondered. Could he intend to stand her up? To get even in a small way for the humiliation she had dealt him?

She knew she was being ridiculous. She'd seen no indication that he was that petty a person. And really, he'd given her a dozen roses. That wasn't the action of an angry man. But Ali was really nervous, and her imagination kept coming up with all sorts of ways that this date could go horribly wrong. And one scenario was that this date was never intended to be a real date at all.

The foie gras arrived at the same moment as her loaner shawl, which was a simple thing of black embroidered with tiny seed pearls. It looked like something a rich grandmother would wear, but it was warm and so she wrapped it around her shoulders. Then she guzzled some wine and took a taste of the appetizer. Turned out foie gras was a yellowish-pink paste

that tasted like liver, but wasn't all that bad. She might even
have enjoyed it if her stomach weren't cramping with anxiety.

She'd finished her wine and was contemplating a second
when Ken finally arrived. She was hyperaware of the muted
ding of the elevator and had actually slid around in the booth
so she could see it opening and closing without ratcheting her
head around every time. So she got a good look—even in this
light—at his haggard expression and his sideways-leaning tie.

The maître d' greeted him and smoothly stepped between
herself and Ken, clearly blocking the view. When the two
finally started moving toward the table, Ken's hair was no
longer mussed, his tie was centered and smoothed and even
his expression looked calm—or frozen with panic—it was
hard to tell which.

It didn't matter. She'd seen him come off the elevator looking stressed, and that reassured her as nothing else could. This
hadn't been an elaborate setup to a humiliation. He probably had been hung up in traffic. And, frankly, he was rather
adorable-looking when his hair went every which way. Reminded her of the way he looked after some of their more
adventurous nighttime sex-capades.

But he was smooth and put together when he made it to
the table, even if his first words were an apology.

"I'm so sorry, Ali. I tried to get here as fast as I could, but
I couldn't. I just…" He sighed and held up his hands. "I really
tried."

"It's okay," she said, smiling in relief. "You're here now.
Sit down and try some…uh…"

"Foie gras," supplied the maître d'. "Was it not to your
liking?" he asked.

Ali tried to find the words that wouldn't insult the food
but still wouldn't have her confessing that she'd been too
nervous to eat. But before she could say anything, the man
whisked the food away.

"Never mind. Goose liver isn't my favorite either. While

the gentleman gets settled, I will get you something less…
French." He spoke the words as if *French* was synonymous
with what-were-they-thinking?

Ali felt her lips curve at that, and one glance at Ken's face
had her suppressing a laugh. He obviously didn't know what
to think of such an attitude either.

"I don't even know what foie gras is," he confessed in an
undertone.

"Liver, I believe. With mustard."

"Seriously? That sounds really, really…unappetizing."

"It actually didn't taste that bad. I just…"

"Not your style?"

"Not that hungry."

He stilled for a moment, his expression tightening into disappointment. "Oh. I'm sorry. You're not…hungry?"

"No, no!" she scrambled to say. "Actually, I am hungry. I
just… I mean…" She shrugged and decided to go for broke.
"I'm a little nervous."

He nodded. "Well, then you're doing a lot better than me.
I'm *very* nervous."

"Good." She exhaled, her shoulders easing down with the
motion. Then she caught sight of his face and scrambled to
explain. "Not good that you're nervous. Good that we're both
nervous and that means you're not here to punish me."

He blinked, obviously startled. "Punish? Why would you
think that?"

She looked down at the crumpled linen napkin in her lap.
"I did refuse your proposal of marriage."

"You didn't *know* it was a proposal of marriage." He said
it as though it was his fault that she was so clueless.

She opened her mouth to say something—anything to ease
the tension—but nothing came out. Thankfully, the waiter
appeared asking Ken if he wanted a drink. Then there was
the business of looking at the menu—Ali noticed that hers
didn't even include the prices—and ordering something she

hoped was modest. She picked a simple chicken dish. He ordered a steak and then they were alone again with nothing to say. Fortunately, Ali had thought of something while he'd been looking at his menu.

"The roses are beautiful, Ken. Thank you."

He smiled at her, not the roses. "*You* look beautiful. And I'm glad they got here. I'm sorry I couldn't present them to you myself."

"The maître d' did it just as you would, I'm sure. With flair and panache."

"I'm not sure I could find panache with a GPS, but thank you." Then he sobered. "Let me tell you why I was late. It wasn't on purpose, I swear."

"I never thought it was," she lied. And she noticed thankfully that he looked as if he believed her.

"I was in a meeting with some Hollywood studio guys."

She blinked. "Seriously?"

He nodded. "Yeah, that's exactly what I said when Paul told me they wanted to meet. Turns out one of the studio execs was at the theme park with his kid at the same time we were. They came into the booth because it was hot—"

"Everybody came in because it was hot."

Ken flashed a grin. "I know. That's why we book it whenever we can. Anyway, they came in, talked to us and played the game. Then they bought the game and junior played it with all the other studio-executive kids. Turns out, Winning Guinevere is a hit with the children of studio executives."

Ali grinned. "Of course it is. It's a great game."

"And apparently, they think it will be a great movie."

She blinked, her stomach squeezing tight for an entirely different reason than anxiety. Right then, it was joy. Pure joy. "It will make an incredible movie!"

"I'm not so sure. Games don't always translate well to film."

"But the story base is already there. It doesn't have to be gamelike. It just has to be a good quest story. Which it is!"

Ken smiled. "Well, it sounds like you and Paul agree. As do these guys. They flew out for the day just to talk contract details. They're right now in our conference room eating pizza while Blake's agent tries to squeeze them for extra seconds of title time on his name."

She frowned for a number of reasons. She started with the least important one only because it managed to somehow crowd its way to the front. "They want Blake in the movie?"

"It's low budget. They like him and his work so far, so they're willing to give him a shot assuming he agrees to being paid almost nothing."

She thought about Brian/Blake and knew that money would be the smallest of problems. "He'll want to do it. He wants movie stardom like he wants free hair product."

Ken snorted. "Yeah. Everyone knows that, though he's trying to play it cool."

"I'm so glad for him."

Ken paused, a frown starting to creep between his eyebrows. "They're talking about shooting next summer. He's talking about moving to California. That's okay with you, isn't it?"

She blinked. "Of course it is. Why wouldn't it be?"

Ken flushed and looked down at his fingers drawing circles in the condensation on his water glass. "Oh, well, I just heard that you and Blake got closer—you know, at the end of the tour. Have you two been—"

"Seeing each other?"

He looked up, his cheeks red. "Yeah. Have you?"

"Sure. We had nachos the other day. He needed help with ideas for a present to give his sister." She reached out and touched Ken's cold fingers. "We're just friends, Ken. That's all we ever were."

"Oh. Okay. Good."

Lord, she was handling this badly. But she couldn't find a way to get to the topic they both really cared about: their future relationship. And while she squirmed trying to find a way to get there, something else fitted into her brain.

"Wait a minute. You've got Hollywood types in for the day to negotiate a movie deal with you."

He nodded.

"So what the hell are you doing here with me? Isn't that kind of important?"

He shrugged. "Truthfully, it's awesome, but the business was doing fine even before the offer."

Ali nodded. She'd been watching the game blogs. It turned out that Ken's proposal had indeed hit YouTube, along with the leaked information that it had been a *real* proposal. Not surprisingly, that had sparked a flurry of Team Arthur gamers—all girls. Apparently girls could really get behind a product if properly motivated. Winning Guinevere was a huge success.

And now it was going to go Hollywood! "That's amazing. You're going to have a movie!"

He grinned. "Looks like."

"Assuming you guys agree to terms."

"We have."

"And you schmooze them right."

"Paul's on that right now."

"But *you* should be on that, shouldn't you? Not here with—"

Ken held up his hand, effectively stopping her words. And then he reached out and took her hands in his. "Nothing is more important than being here with you, right now, right here."

"But—"

"No buts, Ali." He swallowed and tightened his grip on her fingers. "Look, I know I screwed up. I know I shouldn't have proposed like that. But it was an honest proposal. I really want to marry you, Ali."

She blinked, startled to discover that her eyes were watering. "Why, Ken? Why do you want to marry me?"

He frowned as if her words made no sense to him. But he answered anyway. "Because I love you. Why else would I propose?"

Why else indeed? God, one look at his face told her that it was so simple for him. He loved her, ergo he proposed. That after everything, *she* was the one who had overthought it. *She* was the one who was jumping from what-if to maybe-this or maybe-that. God, she was such an idiot!

Meanwhile, he misunderstood her silence and tumbled into a babble of words. "I know I screwed up. You're not a geek chick or anything like my sister, who wants her proposal to be nationally televised. I don't know why I thought that. You're a normal girl—a great girl—and what you want—"

"Is a man who loves me. That's all. Just a man who loves me like I love him."

He nodded, his head bobbing up and down. "Right. So I figured we'd date for a while now. In the normal world. No tour."

"Me, too—"

"And then, after a few months—or longer if you need it— we can talk about marriage again. I still have the ring. I can propose to you however you want, whenever you want. I want you to be comfortable—"

"Ken—me, too."

"Good. Because marriage is a serious thing. And I don't want—"

She pushed her hand to his lips. "Ken!"

He shut his mouth and looked at her.

"I said, 'me, too.' As in yes, Ken, I love you, too."

He blinked. Then his eyes suddenly widened. "Me, too? I mean, you, too? I mean—"

"I've been thinking about you nonstop since you left. I know I haven't emailed much."

"You're not one to put stuff in writing like that. You like to internalize things. I get that. I do that, too. Which is why I didn't email much either."

And they hadn't. Just short, clear conversations of about two sentences max.

"But I loved every minute of the summer together. You told me—on stage—exactly what you love about me. Let me tell you what I love about you. You're grounded, Ken, even in a world of fairies, gnomes and barbarian warriors."

"I'm not big on the gnomes. Just an FYI."

She laughed. "And that's another thing. You make me laugh, you take me to amazing restaurants and you haven't said a word about this shawl."

He frowned. "Uh…it's lovely," he began.

"No, it's not. It's a loaner because I was cold, and it looks like Barbara Bush left it here by accident."

He looked around. "Actually, that's a possibility."

"I know it is! But you knew that it was nothing like what I would normally wear."

He shrugged. "It didn't seem like your style at all."

"And you know that. You know that even when I don't really know all of that. Ken, you spent the entire summer challenging me to do more, to be more, to…well, everything more. I'm *more* because of you. That's what I love most about you. You demand more of yourself and of me. And you love me even if I don't measure up."

"Of course you measure up—"

"I won't. Not always."

"And I won't get the right restaurants or propose in the right way all the time either."

She grinned. "Ken, I love you. I was an idiot to refuse you in the first place."

"You were shocked and unprepared."

"And you were feeling awkward and thought hiding behind King Arthur would make it easier to propose."

He looked startled for a moment then shrugged. "Yeah, you're right." Then he frowned. "Will you wear the ring now? Please? I've been dreaming of putting it on your finger since I first got it."

She nodded, pulling back enough to hold up her hand.

He fumbled in his pockets and drew out the jeweler's box, popping it open with speed if not style. Then he pulled the ring out and held it up to the light.

"Ali Flores, will you do me the greatest honor and marry me?"

She bit her lip, feeling the love she had for him well up inside her. They were rushing things. She knew they were. Hell, they'd only had two dates. But inside she knew it was right. So she nodded. "Yes, Ken, I will."

He pushed it on her finger, then scrambled around the table enough to kiss her deep and full, just like she adored. And then he pulled back, glancing up as the maître d' clapped his hands.

"Champagne!" the man cried.

Ali laughed. Now this was a picture-perfect proposal! And then she looked at the ring, twisting it in the light as she inspected it closer. The setting was unusual. The diamond wasn't sitting in the usual prongs, but was settled on what looked like a crown.

"Ken—"

"You don't recognize it, do you?"

"No, what is it?"

"At the end of the game, when Guinevere finally gets her man, she gets a new crown." He pointed at her ring. "She gets one shaped just like that."

"Wow," she whispered.

"It's so you know that you're my queen. You always have been. From the very first moment that I saw you."

"Ken, I'm a flesh-and-blood woman. Don't put me on a pedestal."

He grinned. "Well, then I guess you'll just have to remind me of the more…um…carnal nature of your life."

She laughed. God, she did love his sense of humor. "Agreed," she said. "Though I did enjoy it when you acted as my supplicant."

"For tonight, I'd just like to be your fiancé. Your ecstatically happy fiancé."

"Me, too." Then she leaned over and whispered in his ear, "We'll play tavern wench tomorrow."

"Oh my God, I love you!"

Ali grinned. It was amazing how well the man read her mind.

* * * * *

COMING NEXT MONTH from Harlequin® Blaze™
AVAILABLE OCTOBER 16, 2012

#717 THE PROFESSIONAL
Men Out of Uniform
Rhonda Nelson
Jeb Anderson might look like an angel, but he's a smooth-tongued devil with a body built for sin. Lucky for massage therapist Sophie O'Brien, she knows just what to do with a body like that....

#718 DISTINGUISHED SERVICE
Uniformly Hot!
Tori Carrington
It's impossible to live in a military town without knowing there are few things sexier than a man in uniform. Geneva Davis believes herself immune...until hotter than hot Marine Mace Harrison proves that a military man *out* of uniform is downright irresistible.

#719 THE MIGHTY QUINNS: RONAN
The Mighty Quinns
Kate Hoffmann
When Ronan Quinn arrives in Sibleyville, Maine, he finds not just a job, but an old curse, a determined matchmaker and a beautiful woman named Charlie. But is earth-shattering sex enough to convince him to give up the life he's built in Seattle?

#720 YOURS FOR THE NIGHT
The Berringers
Samantha Hunter
P.I. in training Tiffany Walker falls head-over-heels in lust for her mentor, sexy Garrett Berringer. But has she really found the perfect job *and* the perfect man?

#721 A KISS IN THE DARK
The Wrong Bed
Karen Foley
Undercover agent Cole MacKinnon hasn't time for a hookup until he rescues delectable Lacey Delaney after her car breaks down. But how can he risk his mission—even to keep the best sex of his life?

#722 WINNING MOVES
Stepping Up
Lisa Renee Jones
Jason Alright and Kat Moore were young and in love once, but their careers tore them apart. Now, fate has thrown them together again and given them one last chance at forever. But can they take it?

You can find more information on upcoming Harlequin® titles, free excerpts and more at www.Harlequin.com.

HBCNM1012

REQUEST YOUR FREE BOOKS!
2 FREE NOVELS PLUS 2 FREE GIFTS!

red-hot reads!

*Bestselling Harlequin® Blaze™ author Rhonda Nelson
is back with yet another irresistible Man out of Uniform.
Meet Jebb Willington—former ranger, current security
agent and all-around good guy. His assignment—to catch
a thief at an upscale retirement residence. The problem—
he's falling for sexy massage therapist Sophie O'Brien,
the woman he's trying to put behind bars....*

Read on for a sneak peek at
THE PROFESSIONAL

Available November 2012 only from Harlequin Blaze.

Oh, hell.

Former ranger Jeb Willingham didn't need extensive army training to recognize the telltale sound that emerged roughly ten feet behind him. He was Southern, after all, and any born-and-bred Georgia boy worth his salt would recognize the distinct metallic click of a 12-gauge shotgun. And given the decided assuredness of the action, he knew whoever had him in their sights was familiar with the gun and, more important, knew how to use it.

"On your feet, hands where I can see them," she ordered. He had to hand it to her. Sophie O'Brien was cool as a cucumber. Her voice was steady, not betraying the slightest bit of fear. Which, irrationally, irritated him. He was a strange man trespassing on her property—she ought to be afraid, dammit. Why hadn't she stayed in the house and called 911 like a normal woman?

Oh, right, he thought sarcastically. Because she wasn't a *normal* woman. She was kind and confident, fiendishly clever and sexy as hell.

He wanted her.

And the hell of it? Aside from the conflict of interest and the tiny matter of *her name at the top of his suspect list?*

She didn't like him.

"Move," she said again, her voice firmer. "I'd rather not shoot you, but I will if you don't stand up and turn around."

Beautiful, Jeb thought, feeling extraordinarily stupid. He'd been an army ranger, one of the fiercest soldiers among Uncle Sam's finest…and he'd been bested by a massage therapist with an Annie Oakley complex.

With a sigh, he got up and flashed a grin at her. "Evening, Sophie. Your shrubs need mulching."

She gasped, betraying the first bit of surprise. It was ridiculous how much that pleased him. "You?" she breathed. "What the hell are you doing out here?"

He pasted a reassuring look on his face and gestured to the gun still aimed at his chest. "Would you mind lowering your weapon? It's a bit unnerving."

She brought the barrel down until it was aimed directly at his groin. "There," she said, a smirk in her voice. "Feel better?"

Has Jebb finally met his match? Find out in
THE PROFESSIONAL

Available November 2012
wherever Harlequin Blaze books are sold.